Brody's VOW

**The
Colebrook
Siblings**

NEW YORK TIMES AND *USA TODAY* BESTSELLING AUTHOR

KAYLEA CROSS

Brody's Vow

**Copyright © 2016
by Kaylea Cross**

* * * * *

**Cover Art by
Sweet 'N Spicy Designs**

* * * * *

ISBN: 978-1535422444

Dedication

To all the strong, kickass women out there, and the men who love them.

Author's Note

Dear reader,

If you've already read the **Hostage Rescue Team** series, then you'll be familiar with the main characters in this first book of **The Colebrook Siblings** trilogy.

Many of you have asked me to write a story for Trinity, and she's just so darn intriguing and mysterious that I couldn't say no. She's the most lethal of all the Valkyries. She has to be, because of how close she has to get to her targets. In this story she's in for a huge surprise when a tall, dark and handsome stranger poses the biggest risk to her of all—by threatening her jaded heart.

Happy reading!
Kaylea Cross

Chapter ONE

Trinity hid her revulsion behind an impassive mask as Franco Salvatori slid a proprietary arm around her waist and leaned in to whisper against her ear, his words clear against the backdrop of the crowd. A steady buzz of conversation filled the ballroom, punctuated by laughter. "Ready to get out of here so we can finally be alone?"

Pasting on her best seductive smile in the low lighting, she nodded, edging her body into his just enough so that her breast brushed along the sleeve of his tuxedo jacket. The ballroom was packed with hundreds of D.C.'s richest citizens, yet he'd managed to find a secluded corner that allowed them a modicum of privacy. "I've been waiting for those words all night."

Salvatori's black eyes glittered as they flicked down to ogle the ample cleavage displayed by the bodice of her black velvet evening gown. He licked his lips before meeting her gaze. "You're a sexy little thing."

She gave him a coy look and set her half-finished

flute of champagne on a passing waiter's tray. "You haven't seen anything yet." She let her gaze drop to his groin, where his erection was visible beneath his tux pants, and licked her lips in turn, a hard knot of anger forming in the pit of her stomach.

She couldn't wait to kill him.

Oblivious to the danger she posed, he gave a low chuckle and tightened his grip on her waist, pulling her close, until the front of her body pressed up against his side. She'd perfected her acting abilities well over a decade ago, commanded her body to stay pliant, even lean into his hold. "I'm looking forward to it," he said in a low voice.

"Good," she murmured next to his ear. *But not as much as I am.* She let one hand trail slowly down the center of his chest, the tip of her index finger pausing at each button, then stopping just above his waistband.

Just enough to make him harder, to make him fantasize about the moment when she unbuttoned his pants and slid her hand inside to fist him. But rather than pleasure him, she was far more likely to grab his balls and twist them until he screamed in agony. Evil bastard.

"Because I'm still so very…hungry," she added in a whisper, her lips brushing his ear.

He was sweating lightly, the scent mixing with the strong cologne he used. Even though the smell made her faintly sick to her stomach she made sure to inhale deeply, give a little purr of enjoyment before easing away from him.

She was a master of seducing her targets. Each one was different and each time she made sure she learned their weakness before ever coming near them.

As far as sexual tastes went and despite all the depraved acts his crimes allowed—like sex trafficking and sex slavery—Salvatori was surprisingly average for his social rank and age. He was in his mid-sixties, his marriage was in name only, and he wanted some action on the side with a twenty or thirty-something sex kitten. Nothing too extreme, just a little light bondage and maybe some rough-edged sex that wasn't always consensual.

Not that she'd let things get that far.

She'd crafted this cover carefully over the past few months, giving him the living, breathing fantasy he'd always wanted: a woman as good in the board room as she was in bed. Once she'd known what she needed in order to get close to him, it hadn't been difficult to construct Eva Gregorivich.

Eva had a master's degree in business from Harvard, started her own software business at twenty-one, strategic investments had made her independently wealthy. That she didn't need his money was yet another thing that made Salvatori want her so much. He was far too used to women sidling up to him for that.

Eva had all the money she would ever need, she had experience, and she also had the reputation of a wild streak in bed guaranteed to make Salvatori sit up and immediately take notice. Her fake identity was solid, even having several reputable charities and other philanthropic endeavors to her name.

But there was just enough unknown about her, enough whispers she'd planted in Salvatori's circle, to make her both alluring and mysterious. She was quite proud of the cover she'd constructed. Eva was an irresistible challenge to a man like him—a rich megalomaniac rumored to have made his fortune from illegal arms deals and with a taste for high-priced escorts and single women half his age.

The people who'd hired her either saw him as enough of an embarrassment, or maybe a threat, to warrant hiring her to kill him. With the payout she would receive from this hit, all the meticulous preparation she'd put in over the past few months would pay off in dividends. She'd take the money and give it to programs that would help Salvatori's many victims.

Salvatori deserved to die for all the American military lives he'd cost with his arms deals, and for all the women he'd subjected to a life of sexual slavery. She knew all too well what it felt like to be a man's victim. It would be her pleasure to send him to hell where he belonged.

Trinity cast a sly glance at her unsuspecting target over her shoulder and raised an eyebrow, the tendrils of golden brown hair she'd teased from the coiffed, updo wig caressing her bare shoulders. "You coming?"

His answering leer told her he hoped to be doing exactly that in the very near future.

He was in for quite a surprise.

She didn't wait for him, just walked away with an extra sway in her hips, the long slit in the left side of her dress showing off the length of her bare thigh and calf. Sexy yet elegant, and it concealed the thin garter strapped to the inside of her right thigh. Knowing he'd follow, she headed for the exit of the grand ballroom, noting where his bodyguard, a hulking man dressed in a Louis Vuitton suit, was positioned. She could take him if she had to, but the fewer hiccups tonight, the better.

Tino waited over by the gleaming granite bar in the corner. He hadn't moved from his spot all night, except to shift stools so he could maintain a visual on Salvatori.

He was a constant thorn in Trinity's side on this job. Normally she would have taken Salvatori out by now but his bodyguard cost a mint for a reason. He was a former Mob enforcer and never let his boss out of his sight, even to take a piss. She would have killed him already had it not posed a high risk of exposing her.

No matter. She'd killed tougher targets than this, and she'd come here prepared. If she had to eliminate them both to get this done, so be it. Killing was second nature to her now.

As she walked to the coat check she was aware of everything happening around her. How many people, where they were positioned, what they were wearing. Every sound.

She feigned surprise to find Tino standing behind her when the man at the coat check station handed her the cream, knee-length peacoat she'd worn. "Oh. Hi."

His hard face was expressionless, but distrust clouded his green eyes. "I'll escort you to your car."

She gave him a sweet, but pointed smile. "That won't be necessary, thank you. I'm going with Franco tonight." She turned her smile on her date, who strode toward them, his gaze lingering on her body.

"It's all right, Tino," he told his goon. "I'll be seeing Ms. Gregorivich home later personally. Much later," he added with a smile as he raised her fingers to his lips.

Tino merely grunted and took her elbow in one big hand. "I'll walk her out," he said in a rough voice.

Knowing full well he wanted to check her for weapons, Trinity acquiesced without an argument and accompanied him outside into the chilly April evening air, taking small steps to make him think her dress and spiked heels made it difficult for her to keep up. Suspicious or not, she needed him to see her—Eva—as a little bit helpless.

They passed by the valet station and continued around the side of the swanky hotel to a shadowy spot away from anyone or security cameras.

"I have to check you for weapons. Stand still," Tino said gruffly.

"What?" she asked, putting enough of an appalled tone into her voice to lend her act realism.

He ignored her and began unbuttoning her coat. She

stiffened, made sure to shoot Salvatori an uncertain glance. Her date watched his bodyguard, but didn't interfere as Tino unceremoniously began checking first her coat, doing a thorough inspection of the pockets and lining before moving on to her dress.

Trinity sucked in a breath and made a show of grabbing his wrists as those meaty hands closed over her ribcage, just above her waist. "Hey," she protested, tightening her grip for a moment. She could break his wrists with one quick twist and some carefully applied leverage if she so chose, but that would have to remain only a fantasy for now.

"Quiet." Tino impatiently brushed her hands aside and skimmed his own over her body, pausing to linger at her breasts.

Even though they were in shadow she could tell by the way he touched her—like she was a *thing* instead of a person, a mere object to satisfy his every sexual whim—that he wanted her. It was another reminder that he and Salvatori often shared women, and that his boss liked to watch Tino with the women he hooked up with.

She hid her distaste behind a mask of outrage as he slipped a hand to the slit in her dress and stole beneath it, his fingers curling around the flesh of her left inner thigh. She swatted at his hand. "*Enough.*"

It would be so satisfying to kill him too, once she was done with Salvatori. Though he wasn't her intended target and she wouldn't get paid for it, killing a ruthless thug like him would be an act of service to the world at large.

Those rough fingers squeezed her thigh suggestively for a moment, then dragged upward, stopping at the triangular edge of the G-string she wore.

Eva would *not* like that. "Get your filthy hands off me," she gritted out, shoving at him.

He didn't budge, seemed to take delight in groping

her and the knowledge he was making her uncomfortable. "You're different than his others," he told her. "I can see why he wants to be alone with you so bad." Even in the dimness the look in his eyes made it clear what else he was thinking. *If you want to see what a real man can do for you once he's finished, let me know.*

Barf. Eva would never lower herself to fucking him, especially not so Salvatori could watch. *"Stop,"* she snapped, mock struggling in his grip.

He merely chuckled and skimmed his hand down the inside of her thigh. When he reached the lacy garter he paused before slipping a finger into it and running it around the inside of the band. His fingers paused on the black satin bow and the crystal nestled in its center.

Confident he'd never figure out that the pretty embellishment hid her weapon, Trinity held herself rigid and pushed again at his solid chest. He was over six feet tall, outweighed her by probably a good eighty pounds or more.

She could still take him down right now, even slit that strong throat before he even knew what was happening, had she brought a blade with her. But knives weren't her weapon of choice. Blades were too messy, left too much evidence behind. And there were too many witnesses around anyway. Tonight's job was more important than killing this disgusting pig, no matter how much he deserved it.

After skimming his free hand all the way down to her ankles and checking her black stilettos, he grunted and stood. Salvatori had joined them now. Tino nodded at him. "She's clean."

Trinity clenched her jaw and jerked her arm from his restraining grasp, recoiling a few steps until she could reach for Salvatori. Playing up her need for reassurance. "That was totally uncalled for," she snapped at Tino, managing to sound shaken. "I'm not a piece of meat for him to feel up."

"I'm sorry," Salvatori said, even though she knew he wasn't. "It's become an unfortunate security precaution, I'm afraid. But there's nothing to worry about now, it's done." He curled an arm around her, brought her close to his side and squeezed her in what he probably thought was a comforting embrace. Protecting her, when he was the one who needed protection.

She fought the urge to laugh.

"Don't follow too closely," he told Tino. "I want some private time with Ms. Gregorivich."

And that's going to cost you your life. Satisfaction slid through her.

He nuzzled her temple, his arm still securely around her. "Shall we?"

Nodding, Trinity allowed him to turn her away and walk her to the big black Mercedes waiting for them at the curb. The valet seated her in the passenger side while Salvatori slid behind the wheel. Normally Tino drove his boss to and from these functions but tonight Salvatori wanted her all to himself. She had to make him think they would have sex in his car, because it was the only place she knew for certain that wasn't bugged. Salvatori didn't want anyone keeping tabs on him or overhearing what went on in his private vehicle.

Once the doors shut, a sense of anticipation curled inside her. This was it. What she'd been waiting for.

Only another few minutes. She knew full well Tino would follow them, and probably a lot closer than Salvatori wanted. He might be a fucked-up, misogynistic, criminal pig, but Tino was damn good at his job. She'd have only minutes to kill Salvatori and make her escape.

"So where are you taking me?" she asked as he steered out of the hotel parking lot. They were in the center of D.C., a city with a heavy security presence. Not her first choice of location to carry out a hit, but she could make it work to her advantage. She knew the entire area by heart now, after spending months here, and knew which routes she could use to escape afterward.

"I've got a reservation for us at one of my hotels. In the penthouse suite."

No way in hell was she going there, where he paid his employees well enough to be loyal and turn a blind eye to whatever went on there, and where every room was bugged and monitored.

She made a disappointed sound. "I was hoping we wouldn't have to wait that long." To emphasize the point, she lowered a hand and drew the fabric of the slit in her dress aside, exposing the length of her left leg as they sat at a red light. "Isn't there a secluded spot we could find between here and there?" She drew her fingertips up her thigh, her blood-red nails grazing over her smooth skin. "A kind of...appetizer before the main course?"

The fixated look on Salvatori's face was almost comical as he stared at her bare thigh, practically drooling at the thought of what she was suggesting. "I know a place," he said, and turned at the next stoplight, taking them east, toward the river. Trinity made note of the car that did the same a minute later, knowing it was Tino.

Traffic was light, especially once they left the downtown core. A few minutes later Salvatori pulled into a darkened, deserted alleyway in an industrial section of town and killed the engine. There were no streetlights here, the only illumination coming from the instruments in his dash.

Impatient now that the big moment had finally arrived, he undid his seatbelt and took off his jacket, his breathing already heavy in the quiet interior. "I've been wanting to fuck you for weeks now," he rasped out, any veneer of the civilized businessman he liked people to think he was long gone.

He'd probably wanted her from the first time they'd met, at another gala nearly three months ago. She'd played hard to get until two weeks ago, then trailed him along ever since, to ensure he didn't lose interest and wanted her enough to drop normal security protocols. She was the best in the business for a reason, and damn proud of it.

Trinity gave him a sultry smile and undid her own seatbelt, stretching in her seat, letting him see all the curves he wanted to handle and would never get to. "I hope I'll be worth the wait."

"Oh, you will be," he said. With a groan he reached for her, wrapping a hand around the back of her neck as he leaned across the console and took her mouth in a wet, openmouthed kiss.

She played along, giving him all the right signals, a tiny mewl of want and a wriggle of her breasts against his chest. Immediately he shot out his other hand to cup one of them, and squeezed hard enough to hurt.

There was no cringe of revulsion on her part, no shudder to give her true feelings away. She was in full op mode now, didn't even register the touch as repulsive, just pressure and warmth on her skin, a signal to confirm that he'd bought her ruse completely.

The instant his tongue delved into her mouth, Trinity saw the flash of headlights in the side mirror as a car turned into the alley and parked at the far end, then shut off its lights.

Just like that, everything clicked into place. This was her moment. She was done with this charade and had to use every available second to get away after the deed was done.

She held the back of Salvatori's head with one hand, keeping their mouths fused as she reached for the tiny weapon hidden in her garter. With one decisive jab she plunged the little needle into the side of his neck, injecting the poison directly into his jugular in a move she'd perfected long ago.

He jerked back with a strangled cry and gripped her wrist with bruising force, his eyes wide with shock and the horror of dawning realization, but it was already too late for him. She held that cold, black stare and dropped her mask, let him see her hatred of him and his kind while the poison ran its course. A fast-acting, untraceable poison she'd used plenty of times before.

He tried to rear back, tried to disengage from her embrace as he gasped for air, but it was no use. Trinity stayed locked with him, made it look to Tino or anyone else able to see them from the shadows like they were in a torrid embrace. Her pulse remained steady and she felt not one shred of sympathy for her victim.

Salvatori sputtered, gasped twice more, then went limp in her arms as his heart stopped. Leaning him back in the seat, she paused long enough to check his pulse. Finding none, she replaced the little charm holding the needle back into her garter, disabled the car's dome light, slipped off her heels, exchanging them for the little pair of folding flats she'd tucked into her evening bag.

Leaving him slumped against the seat, she climbed over him and slid out of the far side of the car, using the darkness to her advantage. The shadows and black gown were her only cover as she raced down the alleyway, the thin flats doing little to cushion the soles of her feet. She wasn't out of danger yet, though.

Her pulse skipped at the sound of a door slamming shut behind her. Tino. She wasn't sure whether he'd seen her exit the car or what might have aroused his suspicion, but it was only a matter of seconds before he saw what she'd done. By then, she had to have enough of a head start to lose him.

She turned left, ran faster, a burst of adrenaline slicing through her when his enraged bellow echoed behind her in the alley. "You're dead, bitch!"

To hell with hiding, she was out of time.

She ran across the street, smashed the window of the first car she came across, and got busy hotwiring it, using another skill she'd been taught years ago. As soon as the engine started she veered away from the curb and raced down the darkened street, leaving headlights off.

A car shot out of the alley she'd just come from, the tires squealing as it turned to follow her.

Trinity pushed down harder on the accelerator and kept going. All she had to do was reach the freeway and she could lose him long enough to ditch this ride for another. Then she'd disappear.

But Tino's car was faster.

No matter how hard she tried, she couldn't lose him. And in a matter of minutes it became clear she wasn't going to be able to outrun him. The realization was humbling, and a little terrifying. Her success rate was one-hundred percent. No one had ever caught her and she didn't intend to let Tino be the first.

The scenery whipped past her in a blur of light and shadow as she sped for the closest freeway onramp, more than a mile away. There was a park on the right, with a lake. Only a few other cars around, and no people that she could see. Her pulse beat faster. She had to get away from him, the alternative was unthinkable.

The headlights in her rearview mirror came closer still.

She ducked instinctively and swerved when the back window shattered. A moment later another bullet slammed into the windshield, leaving a silver-dollar-sized hole.

Trinity swerved again to avoid another shot but he rammed her rear bumper, making her head jerk back against the headrest. She wrenched the wheel to the right at the same moment he rear-ended her again. Her car sailed over the curb and sidewalk, careening straight for the lake.

There was no way to avoid the coming crash.

She barely had time to brace for impact before the wheels hit the damp grass with a bone-jarring thud. The car's back end lifted, sending it airborne. A second later the front end slammed into the water, the force of the collision driving the air from her lungs.

The airbag punched her in the chest and the side of her head struck the window, stunning her. Freezing cold water poured through the shattered back window as the vehicle sank below the surface, shocking her out of her momentary daze.

With frantic hands she undid her seatbelt and shoved the partially-inflated airbag out of the way. The water was already up to her hips and rising fast. But even as she climbed over the seat to escape the sinking vehicle, she knew that Tino would be up there, waiting to shoot her.

Her training took over.

She forced herself to stay there, poised in the backseat while the water level rose up to her waist. Then her chest.

She took several evenly spaced, calm breaths, ignoring her body's instinctual flight response. She didn't know how far down she was, or if she'd have enough air to reach the surface. When the icy water was at her chin she sucked in the deepest lungful of air she could, and shot herself through the back window. With one hand she ripped her wig off, letting it float away in the darkness.

Already the cold was numbing her arms and legs.

She swam upward at an angle, trying to put as much distance between her and the shore as possible before she surfaced. The instant she came up for air, she'd be a target.

The wet velvet of her dress tangled around her legs as she kicked, fighting her way upward. When her lungs burned so badly she feared they were about to burst, she gave a final surge of strength and broke through the water.

She dragged in a ragged breath and immediately went back under, heading for the opposite shore. Above her the crescent moon was hidden behind the clouds, giving her extra cover and leaving her in an inky, watery darkness.

By the time she'd made it to the other side, she was freezing and exhausted. Cold water sluiced off her, weighing down her steps as she dragged herself onto shore and up the grassy bank toward the band of forest surrounding this side of the lake.

Her head throbbed from where it had hit the window and warm blood trickled down the left side of her face. She was shivering, her teeth chattering, hypothermia the most urgent threat to her safety. A glance over her shoulder showed Tino outlined by the thin moonlight on the opposite bank, sliding back into his car.

He wasn't giving up. He was coming after her again. And he had the advantage now that he knew she was a hitter—numerous connections within the Mob and criminal underworld. An entire network of people as lethal as him that he would activate, while she had no one to back her up. She'd known the risks when she'd signed the contract.

Tino would be relentless in his hunt, and if he caught her, he'd make her death slow and painful. Once again, she was on her own, and for the first time she wished she wasn't. But given how woozy the head injury had left her and how fast the cold was sapping her strength, would she finally be caught this time?

She'd lost her shoes in the water. Twigs and branches scraped her bare feet as she ran into the trees, the world a dizzying blur of gray. Her teeth chattered, her body sluggish with the cold but she couldn't afford to stop, not even for one moment.

Already she was thinking about her next move, pushing her numb and exhausted body forward. She'd have to steal another car before Tino found her but there was no way she could go back to the apartment she'd been renting, not even to grab her go bag that held her weapons and documents. Now more than ever she needed backup, someone to have her back until she could treat her injuries and slip out of town.

Except she always worked alone.

Her racing mind flipped through a list of possible places for her to go, and dismissed all of them—except one.

There was only one person she could reach out to now, only one place she might be able to get to that would be safe, but it meant putting people she cared about at risk.

At the moment, however, she didn't see any other way. Her choices were either go there, or die.

Trinity rushed through the trees, determined to make it to Quantico before Tino caught her.

Chapter TWO

Special Agent Brody Colebrook exited the physical rehab facility with a sigh of pure relief and paused on the sidewalk to take a moment, breathing in the sense of newfound freedom.

The early spring evening air was chilly, but so fresh compared to what he'd been breathing for the past ninety minutes during his physical therapy session. His last for the next two weeks, marking the end of a series of surgeries and rehab stints since he'd been wounded in late January. Now he was finally free to head home to the Shenandoah Valley for some serious R&R and he couldn't wait to get there, to unwind and put this all behind him.

His left leg was weak and it ached like a bitch, the constant pain sharper right now because of the workout he'd just put it through. He hid a wince as he stepped down off the curb and started across the parking lot for his truck, his gait uneven, but hell, at least he was walking.

A bullet had taken a chunk out of his lateral thigh during an op in northern Jordan a couple months ago, but at least the Hostage Rescue Team had saved the two remaining hostages, including Summer Blackwell, the wife of a fellow HRT member. Brody's femur had been cracked but not broken, and though he'd always be missing some muscle mass in his quads and hamstrings, he still had two whole legs.

Unlike another member of his family. His older brother Wyatt had been through hell after being wounded by an IED in Afghanistan, so Brody was all too aware of how lucky he'd been in comparison.

He'd no sooner fired up his truck when his phone rang and he was surprised to see DeLuca's number on the screen. He only ever called about work stuff, and Brody was on indefinite medical leave. "Hey, Commander. What's up?"

"You still near Quantico?" No preamble, no bullshit.

"Yeah, I'm just leaving my last appointment, on my way home for a couple weeks." Where at least his dad was looking forward to seeing him.

"Can I call in a favor first?"

He stilled in surprise. "Sure. What do you need?"

"I'm with Blue Team in Austin right now, and Briar's in L.A." His wife. "I just got a message from my alarm company. Apparently our home security system suddenly went offline a little while ago. Is it storming there?"

Brody looked up into the calm, purpling sky, streaked with bands of clouds and the first stars beginning to appear high above. "No, wind's been calm here all day."

DeLuca sighed and Brody could imagine him taking off his Chargers ball cap to run a hand through his short brown hair. "Maybe it was a power surge or something. Anyway, the alarm company can't seem to turn it back on or reset it remotely. Would you mind swinging by our place on the way out of town to check it out? It's probably nothing, but it's weird that the entire system just crashed. The alarm company sent the cops over but they didn't see anything wrong. I'd feel better if I had someone I trust run by to take a look, and I didn't want to ask my neighbors in case there was an actual break-in or something."

"Sure, no problem, I'll stop by now. You got a spare key hidden somewhere?" When he had the information he needed he assured DeLuca he'd call once he checked things out, then hung up. It kind of annoyed him that his trip home would be delayed, but his commander had never asked him for anything and as far as favors went, this was small. Shouldn't take him long and then he'd be on his way.

It took him just under fifteen minutes to drive to his commander's place, a two-story house in a nice, quiet area full of tidy yards and homes. When he pulled up at the curb in front of the house the first thing he noticed was that all the lights were off, even the exterior front porch light, which DeLuca told him he left on whenever he and Briar were both out of town. The cops were long gone.

Before exiting the truck Brody reached into the backseat and withdrew his pistol from the bag he'd packed, tucked it into the waistband of his jeans. He swept his gaze over the front of the property as he approached the house, moving along the side of the yard, near the privacy fence.

He'd been here a handful of times before with his teammates and the guys from the assault team for cookouts in the backyard. DeLuca liked to get the sniper team and assault team guys all together for some social downtime a couple times a year, and so the wives and girlfriends could meet up and get to know one another too.

They didn't get the chance to do that kind of thing often because he and the other guys trained constantly when they weren't on a mission. Their punishing schedule was deliberate, and meant to keep all their skills sharp to protect everyone on the team and ensure they were the best of the best.

That's why he'd been working so hard in the gym and at physio these past two months, to try and regain every bit of function and strength possible in his leg. He was thirty-four, still had a few years of eligibility left on the team.

Whether or not he'd ever be operational again was still up in the air at the moment, and he hated that uncertainty. He wanted to be back with his guys, back in the action, leading from the front as he'd always done, both with the HRT and back during his days in the Corps.

It had been months since he'd felt useful to anyone, and really, doing this favor for his commander was a welcome change of pace. Now he put all his training and experience into use, and damn, it felt good to slip into operational mode again, instead of sitting around on his ass doing nothing. If someone had broken into the house and was dumb enough to still be there, they'd be sorry.

From his vantage point near the fence he could see that the front and garage doors didn't appear to have been tampered with, and all the windows at the front of the house were intact. He continued along the east side, checking for footprints in the damp grass and finding none. At the side entrance to the garage, he paused to inspect the door. Both the knob and the lock showed no signs of forced entry, so he went around the back.

A slight prickle at his nape registered when the security lights mounted on the side of the house didn't go on as he rounded the rear of the house. They were motion-sensored. He remembered them from a former team gathering here. Even with the power being off, they should have come on because they had backup batteries in them.

At the back door, located on ground level next to the stairs that led up to the back deck and into the kitchen, he stilled when he noticed dark splotches on the concrete stoop.

Drawing his weapon, he crouched down for a better view, ignoring the sharp protest from his injured leg. There were definite partial, wet footprints outlined there, as though someone had stood here on tiptoe recently, either barefoot or in socks. But when he glanced up to check for signs of forced entry, again the doorknob and window appeared untouched.

He pushed to his feet to look up at the sliding glass doors that separated the kitchen from the upstairs deck just in case, but didn't see anything suspicious there either. So, back door it was. He was sure whoever had come here was long gone by now, but just in case...

After retrieving the spare key from the hiding spot DeLuca had told him about, he carefully slid it into the lock and used the bottom of his T-shirt to grip the knob so he didn't erase any fingerprints. The door cracked open a few inches, releasing a slight breath of air tinged with gun oil and leather.

But no series of beeps indicating the alarm was on and had registered the door opening.

On guard, Brody stepped into the game room with his weapon aimed dead ahead, and swept the area. Nothing caught his eye or seemed out of place but when he looked down, he instantly spotted the wet footprints gleaming in the dim light on the hardwood floor.

Son of a bitch.

Easing the door shut behind him, Brody kept his

pistol up and headed through the room in the darkness, moving by memory toward the doorway that led into the downstairs hall. He paused to one side of it, waited a few beats, then whipped around the corner, checking the long, narrow space. Empty, but with the streetlights shining through the transom windows on either side of the front door, he saw the trail of wet footprints continuing down the hallway.

His shoes were silent against the hardwood as he cat-walked his way toward the door, staying close to the wall as he moved. Just as he neared the landing at the bottom of the stairs, a cold female voice came from the shadows to the right.

"Stop right there and drop your weapon."

He whirled then froze at the sight of the woman standing there, the pistol in her grip pointed directly at his chest.

Trinity aimed the Glock at the intruder's center mass, her finger securely around the trigger even though she felt frozen to the core and she could barely keep her teeth from chattering. He was tall, built, and he'd been favoring his left leg as he moved. If he was one of Tino's contacts, it didn't make sense that he hadn't tried to shoot her yet.

"Put it down, now," she ordered in a low voice when he didn't move, the ache in her head hurting worse as she spoke.

"You first," he shot back, his stance and posture just as unyielding as hers.

In the light coming through the thin, rectangular windows on either side of the front door, he looked wary but not afraid and right away she recognized that he was a seasoned operator. Somewhere in his thirties, he had short dark hair and dark whiskers on his square jaw. And his gaze never wavered from hers.

"Not happening," she said, survival instinct making her alert in spite of her injuries and fatigue.

"Who the hell are you, and what are you doing in here?" he demanded, a distinctive Virginia drawl lacing his voice.

She didn't know who he was, but figured if he'd been sent here to kill her, they wouldn't be having this conversation because one of them would already be dead. A sobering thought. "You first."

"Special Agent Brody Colebrook, FBI. Now why the fuck are you in my commander's house?"

So he was HRT. She vaguely recognized his name from a past conversation with Briar, remembered he was on one of the sniper teams. She relaxed a fraction. Just because he was HRT didn't mean she trusted him one hundred percent, but he obviously wasn't going to shoot her unless he had to.

So she lowered her weapon a little. Slowly.

Colebrook didn't move, just stared at her and waited, pistol still aimed at her. "Well?"

"I'm a friend of Briar's."

Surprise flashed across his face, then he unhurriedly lowered his weapon to match her stance. They remained edgy, both of them still holding their pistols in a double-handed grip. "Prove it."

She mentally laughed. "I can't. You'll just have to take my word for it." She couldn't call Briar for proof because she didn't have a phone with her.

His lips twisted into a hard, cynical smile. "I don't think so." He lowered his weapon a few more inches, switching to a one-handed grip as it rested alongside his right thigh. Then he raised his left hand and held it at shoulder level, palm out in a nonthreatening gesture. "I'm going to pull my phone out of my front pocket and call my commander to verify," he said, watching her intently. "If you're who you say you are, we'll go from there. If not…" He let the unfinished threat dangle but she wasn't worried. If he called his commander, Matt would vouch for her.

"Fine, but put it on speaker." She watched his every move as he retrieved his phone and dialed someone. If it was the cops instead of Matt, she'd shoot him in the good leg and be long gone before anyone could follow her.

"Hey, it's me," he said when Matt answered. "I found out why your security system isn't working." In the silvery light coming through the windows his eyes gleamed darkly as he pinned her with a hard gaze. "Someone disabled it. She says she's a friend of Briar's. Didn't give me a name and now we're both standing here in your front entryway having a Mexican standoff. Want to help me out?"

"This is Supervisory Special Agent DeLuca," Matt said, his voice echoing in the stillness. "Who am I speaking to?"

"It's Trin," she replied, relief spilling through her at the sound of his voice, a heavy weight of fatigue flooding in.

A beat of surprised silence passed. "Trin? What are you doing there?"

"I…ran into a snag and needed somewhere to stay." She'd been hoping for backup, and not in the form of the man facing off with her right now.

"Damn," he muttered. "Colebrook, it's okay. Trinity's an old friend of Briar's."

Colebrook grudgingly tucked his weapon into the back of his waistband and Trinity set hers on the table behind her. The moment she did, a wave of dizziness and exhaustion hit her as the night and head injury caught up to her. She steeled herself, refused to let her guard down and collapse onto the chair behind her the way her body was begging to. She'd been through far worse than this before, and would never let him see how tired and hurt she was.

Letting out a slow breath, she stepped out of the shadows, careful to stay away from the transom windows in case Tino or anyone from his deadly network had managed to follow her here, and let Colebrook see her.

The FBI agent straightened, a frown pulling his eyebrows together when he took in the sight of her, dressed in too-tight jeans and sweater she'd snagged from Briar's closet, her wet hair plastered to her head and the blood streaking down the side of her face and neck. Her head ached like hell and she was pretty sure she needed a stitch or two in her scalp.

"What the hell's going on?" he demanded.

"What's wrong?" Matt said, his voice sharp.

"Nothing," Trinity answered quickly, giving Colebrook a warning shake of her head, covering a wince as a sharp pain lanced through her skull and her sore neck muscles protested. Matt would already have figured out that she was in trouble but she wasn't giving him details. He would get other people involved if she told him, and she didn't want anyone's help but Briar's.

There was no one else she could go to for assistance. She hadn't had time to get a new phone and there was no landline in the house. As per usual she was all on her own on this one, no handler, no backup of any kind. It was what made her so good at her job and why various organizations and agencies hired her to fulfill certain contracts—she had no ties to trip her up, giving her the flexibility to operate on her own and make her own decisions. This was the way she'd always operated, ever since leaving the Valkyrie program, and normally she loved the freedom.

At times like this, however, it was a damn lonely and dangerous place to be.

She also didn't want anyone else put in danger because of her, and she'd learned a long time ago that she couldn't rely on anyone but her Valkyrie sisters. So, it was Briar or nothing. "Look, we're good now. Where's Briar?"

"L.A."

Crap. No reinforcement for her anytime soon then. She covered her disappointment. "Tell her I said hi. Sorry about the break-in—I'll set the security system again before I leave."

"Nuh-uh, you didn't break into my house and disable my very expensive, state-of-the-art security system just to see if you could. So what's going on?" he demanded.

"Really, I'm fine." Or she would be, as long as she could get out of the area undetected and take a few days to recover before trying to leave the country.

But she couldn't get on a flight without one of her IDs, and they were all stashed back at her rental apartment. Which was the first place Tino would look once he started digging into her background, and all his various law enforcement contacts would help him.

"Trin. Just tell me. I can help you," he said, his tone impatient.

No you can't. And he could push all he wanted, but she wasn't telling him anything, least of all with Colebrook here. She didn't trust the agent standing in front of her. "It's all good now. I needed a change of clothes so I borrowed some stuff from Briar." Man, her friend was skinny. The jeans were damn near cutting off her circulation and the sweater kept riding up.

"Who's after you?" he pushed.

"Matt. Leave it alone."

He expelled a loud breath, clearly irritated by her stubbornness. "All of you are the fucking same," he grumbled, and there was no mistaking he meant her,

Briar and Georgia, all former Valkyries. "You guys drive me insane more often than not, you know that? It's no wonder I'm going bald."

"Having one thinning spot on the top of your head is not the same as going bald." She had her reasons for being stubborn about this, and she was sticking to them.

He grunted. "I gotta go. But if you need anything— I don't care what it is—call me. In the meantime, you can trust Colebrook. I'll tell Briar you were looking for her."

Trust Colebrook? She didn't think so. She didn't trust anyone until they'd earned it. "Thanks. I might be out of touch for a few days. Tell her I'll call her once I get back to London."

"I will." Matt gave a hard sigh. "Colebrook, take me off speaker."

Trinity stiffened as he did just that, listened to Matt for a few moments then mumbled a response and ended the call. The sudden silence filled the space until it pressed in on her from all sides. "What did he say?" she demanded.

"That you insisting you're *fine* is bullshit, and that I'm supposed to help you in whatever way I can and watch your back until you're safe."

She clenched her jaw and narrowed her eyes, hating that Matt saw her as needing that kind of help. Even if at the moment, she actually did.

"So, Trinity," Colebrook said, taking an uneven step toward her. "Want to tell me what the hell happened to you tonight?"

Before she could blurt out the lie waiting on the tip of her tongue, the sound of a car engine racing up the street caught her attention. She tensed, her head automatically turning toward the door, and stood there listening for a few seconds. The sound grew louder with every heartbeat. Coming closer.

Tino. He'd found her somehow. She had only seconds before he opened fire.

On pure instinct she launched herself at Colebrook, wrapping her arms around his waist as she tackled him to the floor, trying to make them as small a target as possible. A loud bang from outside echoed in her ears as they fell.

He let out a pained grunt as they hit the hardwood, then automatically rolled to place her in front of him so that her back pressed against the wall, shielding her with his larger body. She stayed rigid, her bleeding head pressed to his chest, tensing for impact.

But when no bullets tore through the windows or wall, her hammering heart began to calm and it slowly dawned on her that it hadn't been a gunshot she'd heard. It had been nothing but an engine backfiring.

She didn't even have time to feel relieved or embarrassed before Colebrook suddenly rolled her beneath him, his hard, muscular frame crushing her into the hardwood, her wrists caught in his iron grip as he pinned her hands above her. He loomed over her in the shadows, a foreboding expression on his chiseled face.

His dark eyes locked on hers, full of quiet fury as he bit out, "All right, I've had enough. You better start talking. Fast."

Chapter THREE

Brody might not know who the woman he had pinned to the floor was, or what had happened to her, but he *was* sure of two things. One, she had amazing curves. And two, he was pretty sure she thought someone was out to kill her.

She glared up at him with a mutinous expression ruined by the streaks of blood marring the left side of her face, and refused to say anything. The skin of her wrists was freezing.

"Start talking," he snapped, out of patience. She'd just fucking tackled him to the floor as though she'd been expecting someone to open up on the house when that car backfired.

She huffed out an irritated breath as though *she* was the one who had the right to be annoyed. "I'm like Briar."

"What do you mean, *like* her?"

"A Valkyrie."

That meant nothing to him, but it also made him

insanely curious. He knew Briar was pretty badass in her own right, knew she could shoot a rifle damn near as well as he and DeLuca, which was saying something. As to what other training she had or what her background was, he didn't know. If Trinity had that same type of training, then he had a whole new level of respect for her.

Except right now, he just wanted answers and to find out what kind of danger she—and now he, because of her—was facing. "Who's after you?"

Her jaw clenched once before she grudgingly answered. "A hit man."

Ah, just fucking great. "Who specifically?"

"Former Mob enforcer."

Jesus H. Christ. He ground his back teeth together as he stared down at her. Her skin was pale, almost translucent, her short dark hair plastered to her head and her eyes ringed by smudged dark makeup.

He released his hold on her wrists, eased up onto his forearms but refused to give her any more space than that. "What did you do, kill somebody?"

If possible, her gaze grew cooler. Rather than answer, she shrugged.

Shit, really? He couldn't see DeLuca vouching for her and being so concerned for her welfare if she was a criminal, so it had to be a sanctioned hit of some kind. "What happened to you?"

"My car crashed into a lake."

What? His eyebrows shot upward, but he guessed her answer explained the water he'd seen on the floor and why her hair was still wet. He eased up more, covering a wince as he got to his knees. "Here," he said, offering a hand to help her up.

She rebuffed the offer, pushing his hand away as she sat up and scrambled out from underneath him, giving him a close-up view of the jeans clinging to the shapely curve of her ass.

He shoved to his feet, set a hand on the wall to steady himself as his leg protested. Son of a bitch, his night wasn't going at all the way he'd hoped. "You hurt?"

"I'm fine." Her voice was every bit as cold as her skin had been.

"You're bleeding," he pointed out.

She didn't answer, just swept past him on her way to the foot of the stairs. "Since Briar's not in town, I'll just borrow another change of clothes for the road and leave."

"But he's still out there, looking for you."

Trinity paused on the lower stair and turned her head to meet his gaze. The weak light coming in from either side of the door showed her delicate features. And dammit, he might not know who she was but he couldn't just let her leave if she was in danger. Not if she was a friend of Briar's and DeLuca's. His boss had asked him to look out for her and Brody wasn't about to abandon her.

"Where will you go?" he pressed when she didn't say anything.

She gave a tight shrug that told him it was none of his business. "I'll manage."

Annoyed by the brushoff when he was just trying to help, he followed her up the stairs. "Trinity."

She stopped, her posture stiff, and didn't turn to look at him.

"I don't know what the hell you're into here, but if you came looking for Briar then you obviously need help. DeLuca asked me to do what I can, so—"

"I don't need your help." And with that, the ice-princess swept up the stairs, leaving a trail of frost behind her.

The smart thing to do was just turn around and walk

away. Head out to the street, climb into his truck and drive for the Shenandoah without looking back, leaving her and whatever mess she was in behind him.

Except dammit, he didn't work that way.

"Damn stubborn woman," he muttered to himself, climbing the last of the stairs just as Trinity disappeared into the master bedroom. His thigh was beyond pissed at him, the ache bone-deep. He stayed in the hallway, leaned back against the wall and crossed his arms over his chest. "What's a Valkyrie?"

A soft snort answered him, from the depths of the walk-in closet. "That's above your pay grade and security clearance."

Nice. He scowled. Who the hell was she? Why had she come for Briar's help, specifically? Trinity obviously trusted her a lot. Damn, it stung his pride to have her refuse his offer of assistance. If she knew he was one of DeLuca's guys, then she knew what sort of training he had. It was as though she didn't trust his abilities.

"You know, as far as help goes, I'm not a bad guy to have around in a tight spot." Even with a bum leg he was a hell of a lot better protection for her than nothing.

Hushed footsteps came toward him. A moment later Trinity appeared in the bedroom doorway, dressed in that snug sweater, the jeans looking like she'd painted them on, a pair of running shoes on her feet. Her short, inky hair was tucked back behind her ears and she'd rubbed away most of the blood from her face and neck but some still trickled down from her hairline.

"Look, it's nothing personal, but I don't know you." She wiped absently at the blood on her temple and he frowned, reached out to catch her wrist when he saw how much blood was on her fingers. She was bleeding worse than he'd realized.

Trinity froze at his touch, and goose bumps rose on

her forearm. Her skin was freezing.

This was ridiculous and he wasn't going to stand here and let her bleed or pass out from hypothermia. "Come here," he ordered, and began dragging her toward the hall bathroom. She resisted at first but he just pulled harder and she gave in with an annoyed huff.

In the bathroom he shut the door then flipped on the lights. She winced and squinted at the sudden brightness. When she opened her eyes and stared up at him, Brody got his first good look at her.

She appeared to be in her early to mid-thirties. Her eyes were a vivid, dark blue, surrounded by inky black lashes. Her hair was blue-black, cut into a sharp, jaw-length bob. The top of her head came up to his mouth, and blood welled from a gash in her scalp. Bruises were forming on the left side of her face as well, and it made him wonder what other injuries she had that he couldn't see.

She stared right back at him, her expression and the tilt of her chin full of defiance. "I can take care of myself."

Maybe, maybe not. And with a Mob assassin and his network targeting her, Brody didn't like her chances going out alone. "You're not going to be able to treat that slice properly by yourself."

"I was going to take care of it before I left."

He grasped her cold chin in his hand, stared into her eyes as he assessed her. Her pupils were evenly dilated but she'd taken one hell of a bump to the head. "You dizzy? Sick to your stomach?"

She pushed his hand away, gave him an impatient look. "No."

"Fine, then let me stop the bleeding at least."

She held his stare for another long moment then gave in, folding her arms over those luscious breasts and angling her body so that he could see the cut better.

Brody opened the mirrored-medicine cabinet door above the sink and took the medical kit from the glass shelf. He grabbed a facecloth and ran it under some warm water, wrung it out before turning back to her.

"This is gonna sting," he warned.

"Fine, go for it," she said in a resigned tone.

Alrighty then.

He carefully parted her hair to get a better look at the gash. It was over two inches long, and resting atop a big goose egg in her scalp. He dabbed at it as gently as he could to clean the dried blood away but more welled up and trickled into her hair. "I'm gonna put antibiotic cream on it then use some liquid suture to close it."

She didn't answer so he got to work, pinching the edges of the wound together so he could squeeze the adhesive onto her skin. He held it there until it dried, then slowly released his grip. She hadn't flinched or made a sound the entire time. "It's holding for now, but you should definitely get this looked at and take it easy for a while."

She moved away from him immediately and reached for the doorknob, paused to steady herself. "Thanks."

Hell. If she left with that head injury, he was worried she'd wind up dead. He expelled a harsh breath. "What's the chance this Mob enforcer or any of his friends followed you here?"

"Less than five percent," she answered without missing a beat.

"For real. I need to know the truth on this."

"That is the truth. I switched vehicles twice after getting out of the lake and I'm sure no one followed me."

Yet she wasn't so certain about that, since she'd tackled him to the floor a few minutes ago. "How *did* you get out of the lake, by the way?"

"I swam."

"You—" Brody stopped and smothered a dry chuckle as he imagined the scene playing out in his head. The car careening over the bank and into the water, her escaping the sinking vehicle and swimming for shore, then stealing two different vehicles and finding her way here. All the while suffering from near hypothermia and a head injury. He was becoming less annoyed and more intrigued by the woman every minute.

Trinity twisted the knob, jerked the door open.

"I'm heading out of town to visit my family," he said, hoping he wouldn't regret this later. "Not far, just a couple hours away in the Shenandoah Valley. You could come with me."

She swiveled her head around, the motion stiff, and shot him an incredulous look. Just as quickly, her expression turned guarded. "Why would you offer that?"

Because he was invested now and she was in trouble so he couldn't walk away. "It's pretty clear you need to get out of here for a while, and I have training. You'll be safe if you're with me. And you just said the chances are next to nothing that anyone followed you here, so my family won't be at risk."

And, okay, he'd be straight up lying to himself if he didn't admit he found her attractive and mysterious. That wasn't why he was offering though. Bottom line was, he just…needed to protect her.

"That's a pretty big gamble to take, considering you don't know me."

He dipped his head in acknowledgment. "I guess it is, yeah." But his dad and eldest brother were the only ones at home, and they were both former Marines. Even if trouble did somehow follow them, though Brody would do everything in his power to make sure it didn't, they could protect themselves.

Those deep blue eyes studied him for a long moment, as though he was a puzzle she was trying to figure out. They were lined with exhaustion and pain, her lips pressed tight together. She was hurting, no matter how much of a tough front she was putting up. "You got a white knight complex or something? I'm not looking for a hero. Because I've got training too, and believe it or not, I can look after myself."

Maybe, but from where he was standing, she was vulnerable at the moment. He couldn't just leave her here when she was in trouble. "Look, the offer's sincere. No strings attached. You're hurt and you've obviously been through a lot tonight. You need to get out of town, and I'm going anyhow. We don't know each other and you might not trust me, but Briar and DeLuca do. That's gotta carry at least some weight with you."

She considered his words for a full minute before looking away and leaning against the door in a clear sign that she was feeling a lot weaker than she'd let on. Then her posture eased. When she looked at him again something like relief filled her eyes as she gave a slight nod. "Okay then, I accept. I…thank you."

He'd been expecting to have to put up more of an argument. He blinked, then put the medical supplies away. Maybe she was planning to ditch him once they got out of town.

When he left the bathroom she was waiting at the master bedroom door…with a rifle in her hands.

"You got more than that pistol with you?" she asked, and the way she held the rifle made it clear she was no stranger to handling one. That made her even more sexy and intriguing.

He looked up and met her gaze. "In my truck, yeah."

"Good." Apparently satisfied by his answer, she headed down the stairs and out to his truck, maintaining careful vigilance as she walked.

As he pulled away from the curb, he checked his mirrors to make sure no one seemed to be following them. What the hell had he just gotten himself into? All he'd wanted after so many months of pain and grueling therapy was some downtime back home to relax and unwind.

Glancing at the intriguing woman in the passenger seat, it looked like his plans for his long-awaited vacation had all just gone up in smoke.

****

Tino slammed a hand down on the steering wheel and cursed in frustration as he came to yet another dead end. He'd followed a third tip from a local detective about a stolen car, but it turned out to be a couple of punk kids taking a joyride.

Where had that bitch gone? He'd seen her crawl out of the lake, had tried to follow but she'd managed to slip out of the thin band of forest and escape him. That had been hours ago, plenty of time for her to get out of the city.

He didn't care what kind of training she had, she couldn't run far or fast enough to escape him. She couldn't stay hidden for long, not with the resources he had at his disposal.

One of the great benefits of belonging to the organization he did was that they had people in virtually every law enforcement agency in the city on their payroll. Big fish, little fish, didn't matter. Everyone had their price, especially in a place like D.C.

He'd already called in a few favors and had some friends out looking for her. Some professional hitters, several cops, even an undercover federal agent who had access to a constant stream of information no one else did. It was only a matter of time before someone found her and alerted him.

They all knew not to kill her after they captured her. That would be his pleasure only, and they all knew what would happen to them if they defied that edict. His predecessor had been tortured for hours before having weights tied to his feet and being dumped into the Potomac. By him.

In his world, reputation was everything. He had to salvage his immediately.

A black wave of rage hit him again as he remembered finding Salvatori slumped in the seat of his Mercedes in that alley a few hours ago. He'd warned Salvatori about Eva right from the start—though he was damn sure that wasn't her real name—had told him she wasn't to be trusted. She'd showed up on the scene out of nowhere, even though her story and persona had checked out.

His boss had laughed off his concerns. Their intensive background check on her had come back clean, the only reason Salvatori had decided to pursue her, but Tino had always felt a certain disquiet around her. Something in her eyes had made him suspicious that she was more than she seemed, that she was duping them all, silently laughing at them and plotting the entire time.

And he'd been right.

Now Salvatori was dead, and Tino was in jeopardy of losing everything he'd worked for these past seven years. With Salvatori he'd finally had the security of a stable job, a steady income, and benefits like a million-dollar condo with a water view, and free pussy whenever he wanted it. All gone now, and that wasn't the worst of it.

He'd gotten used to having excess money to play with, to buy whatever he wanted. Weapons, drugs, women, anything that suited his mood. Over the past eighteen months he'd racked up a sizeable debt living a lavish lifestyle, an amount increased exponentially by a gambling habit he'd become more and more addicted to during his days off.

He'd told himself he could quit anytime he wanted, that he'd be able to pay back the money in no time. The people he owed wouldn't be sympathetic or understanding about his situation, acquaintances and contacts or not. They were the kind of men who would kill him just to make a statement.

And then there was his other problem.

Once everyone found out that Salvatori had died on his watch, Tino's reputation would be in tatters. People within the organization would begin to talk. They'd close ranks, cut him off and shut him out. He'd be ruined, if he wasn't already dead from the bad debt.

Not only that, once Salvatori's boss got wind of this, he might even put a hit order on Tino. When he thought of the sort of people the man would be sending after him…

He shifted against the leather seat as a shiver of unease spiraled up his backbone. That bitch had cost him everything, and he would make her pay. Someone had sent her to kill Salvatori, and once he captured her, he'd find out who. And why.

Tino imagined standing in the shadows beside her earlier, back beside the hotel. He tightened his fingers around the steering wheel as he drove back to his luxury condo.

He'd had his hand between her legs, wished now that he'd simply taken what he'd wanted despite Salvatori's order to wait, make her lose that haughty edge as he taught her she was nothing more than just another slut for him to use for his own pleasure. He'd been hard, even harder than he was now, thinking about the things he would do to her.

Soon enough.

The only way to redeem himself now was to hunt her down and kill her personally. Salvage his rep by proving to the others that *no one* fucked with him or anyone he worked for and lived to tell about it.

Tino sped down the darkened road, a new obsession taking root. He wanted to know who she was. Her name, her background, who she worked for.

And when he finally got her, he was going to take that delectable body, tie her to a bed somewhere and enjoy her for hours on end while extracting every last ounce of information he needed before killing her. She wouldn't be easy to break, not someone with her level of training, but that only made him look forward to the challenge more.

When that day came, he wouldn't make her death quick *or* kind.

Chapter FOUR

As far as decisions went, Trinity was pretty sure this might be one of her worst, but if Briar and Matt both trusted Colebrook, then she was at least safe with him. For the time being anyway.

Logic dictated that things could be worse, however. At minimum he had serious training and would be vigilant. A definite bonus for her at the moment, considering the way she felt. She wasn't bleeding anymore but her head was pounding and her neck and left shoulder were so stiff and sore she could barely move them. On top of that, she was tired enough that if she closed her eyes she was sure she'd drop off to sleep in a matter of moments.

She couldn't afford to let her guard down that far. The jacket she'd pilfered from Briar's closet was waterproof but not overly warm, and even with the sweater she had on underneath it, she was still cold.

Colebrook must have noticed her wrapping her arms around herself because he reached over to aim an air vent at her and cranked the fan up to high. A burst of warm air hit her, and she almost groaned in relief. "Thanks." It felt wrong to be accepting help, let alone from a stranger.

"Welcome."

The silence wasn't awkward, just a bit uncomfortable. She was an expert at putting people at ease though, making them drop their guard on a job. This wasn't a job but she could make an effort to be pleasant after all the trouble he was going to for her. "So where are we headed?"

"Shenandoah Valley. Ever been there?"

"No." It was only a couple hours outside of D.C. though. "Where abouts?"

"Little place called Sugar Hollow."

She barely kept from making a face. "It sounds like something from one of those romantic movies on the Hallmark Channel." The ones she always rolled her eyes at because they were so ridiculously unrealistic and…sweet. No one knew better than her that the real world didn't work that way.

A grin curved his mouth, giving his face a sexy roughness that she found way too appealing. "Romantic isn't the word I'd use, but okay." He shrugged. "It's home."

She kept pulling on the thread of conversation to fill the void. "How long have you been with the HRT?"

"Five years. How long have you been in your line of work?"

The phrasing made her fight a sardonic smirk. As if she'd chosen her profession. Or had a choice at all. "A long time." They'd begun training her at age nine, but hadn't unleashed her on her first target until she was eighteen. Her first kill had been a double agent with a penchant for teenage girls. She'd poisoned him during a private dinner at his house, using her favorite method

41

because it was fast and untraceable.

Trinity glanced in the side mirror again. The road spilled out behind them like a black ribbon. None of the headlights she'd seen had come close enough for her to get a look at the vehicles.

"We're not being followed." His tone was calm, assured.

She turned her head to look at him, gasped and put a hand to her neck as her muscles seized, sending a streak of pain down to her shoulder and up to her jaw. If she was this sore already, tomorrow was going to be ugly. She couldn't let it slow her down. "You're sure?"

"I'm sure." He frowned. "You positive you don't want to get checked out at a clinic or something?"

"Yes." No way was she seeking medical help for something so trivial as whiplash and a cut on her scalp. But she was thirty-two now, and she already knew her body was going to take longer to heal than it would have even a few years ago.

Not for the first time she questioned her sharpness. She might be at the peak of her game in terms of her skill set, but she wasn't getting any younger and wouldn't be able to do this kind of work forever.

The femme fatale role required her to be young and sexy. She'd planned to retire by forty, but now she was second-guessing that. This line of work took a toll on her, mentally and physically. She was weary of hunting. Tired of always having to be vigilant, on guard. Maybe it was time she got out of the game entirely and did something above board.

She'd miss the adrenaline rush, but maybe there was something else that would earn her a decent living, something that wouldn't require her to leave a trail of bodies behind her and having to watch over her shoulder everywhere she went. While she didn't regret killing her targets because they'd all been dangerous criminals of one sort or another, each kill took a piece of her soul with it. In all honesty, she was lucky to still be alive after the life she'd led thus far.

"You can sleep if you want," Colebrook offered.

I don't think so. "Thanks, but I can't."

He eyed her for a second. "Don't trust me to stand watch?"

"It's not that." Except no, she didn't, because she'd just met him. "It's just...ingrained in me not to sleep until after I've gone to ground." Survival instinct overrode everything else. Her training had seen to that.

"I get it," he said with a nod.

Maybe he did. "Did you serve in the military before joining the FBI?"

"Marines."

If he was leader of one of the HRT sniper teams, then he had to be elite. "Are you a scout/sniper like DeLuca?"

He nodded. "One shot, one kill," he said, his voice filled with pride. "What about you? You as good with a long gun as Briar and Georgia?"

She looked at him sharply, narrowing her eyes. "You know Georgia?" Very few people knew her, and fewer still by her real name.

"Met her and Briar on an op in Miami last fall."

Right before Georgia and her new man had disappeared to Cuba together. Interesting. "No, but I can hold my own." She debated how much she should tell him, decided to go for generic. Being a solo contractor had its advantages. As long as she didn't tell him anything classified, she could say what she wanted. "I don't get to kill from afar like she and Georgia do. My specialty is getting up close and personal with my targets."

In any way that required.

Her body and seduction powers were her greatest

lures, as well as formidable weapons. She'd learned long ago how to mentally disassociate during the acts of sex and killing, instead focusing on the power reversal her targets were always unaware of until it was too late.

He shot her a sideways glance but didn't say anything further. She remained alert for the rest of the drive, even though she was nearly certain no one had followed them. By the time they reached Sugar Hollow she had the mother of all migraines going and her body hurt so badly that all she wanted to do was lie down for a few hours.

"We're here," Colebrook murmured a few moments later as he turned into a long, winding driveway off a quiet road in a rural area.

Up ahead in the distance a two-story house stood in the darkness, its lower windows glowing with warm yellow lamplight. "This is your family's place?" She wasn't going to have to make small talk with his parents, was she?

"Yeah, my dad lives here. It's a horse farm. We raise breeding stock."

"What kind of horses?"

"Quarter Horses. They're good at running short distances and can outrun most other breeds in races of a quarter mile or less. That's how they got the name." He parked out front and turned off the truck.

Trinity stifled a pained groan as she got out of the truck before he could come around to help her. Crickets and frogs sang in the background, the scent of fresh cut grass carrying on the light breeze.

Ahead of her the pale yellow farmhouse looked like something out of a painting with its inviting wraparound porch. There was even a porch swing on one end of it, and a couple of rocking chairs near the front door. She pictured Colebrook sitting out here in the evenings with a cold beer. "How many acres of land does your family

44

own?" she asked as he rounded the hood.

"Sixty. It's mostly pasture and woodland."

It was beautiful country. The entire setting was idyllic, the house looking like it should belong to a family in an after-school special. Not the kind of place she ever envisioned visiting.

"Come on, let's get you settled." He started for the porch but she hesitated and he looked back at her. "You're in no shape to go anywhere by yourself tonight," he said in a reasonable tone. "Might as well spend the night here, where you know you'll be safe."

It felt so wrong. Weak. She never relied on anyone to look after her, to protect her, but she had to admit she was in rough shape at the moment, not to mention exhausted.

"Unless you're planning to walk back into town by yourself, come on," he said, heading for the front porch without glancing back.

Her gut said she could trust him. To a point.

Hoping she wouldn't come to regret her decision, Trinity followed him. She stepped into the entryway and gazed around at the homey surroundings as the scents of old wood and lemon greeted her.

Everything was neat and tidy. Wide plank floors stretched as far as the eye could see, leading to a grand wooden staircase that split the lower floor into two halves. The light cream-painted walls made everything appear bright and clean. It was cozy, a home clearly well-loved and cared for by its owner.

Colebrook closed the door behind him and stepped up beside her, and she felt a tug of attraction at having him so close. She put him at around six-two, around two-ten or so. He was wide through the chest and shoulders, and he smelled damn good. Soapy and clean. Good enough that part of her was tempted to lean in and inhale more of his scent.

Which was insane, and maybe she'd hit her head harder than she'd realized. She was so used to using her body to get what she wanted, had never experienced attraction to any of her targets, that this felt...unsettling. And far more tempting than she would have expected.

"You hungry?" he murmured, his quiet tone telling her he didn't want to waken whoever else was at home.

Way hungrier than she should be, under the circumstances, and not for food. That was startling all on its own. It had been...

God, she couldn't remember the last time she'd been attracted to anyone or had sex for pleasure's sake. Had to be nearly two years ago now, that time she'd hooked up with a guy from a pub when she'd first moved to London. And that had only been for one night, after she'd checked him out and looked into his background to make sure he wasn't a threat to her. "No thanks."

"I'll show you up to your room then," he said, heading for the staircase, the hitch in his gait more pronounced than before. Maybe the drive had made his leg stiffen up. "There's some pain meds in the upstairs bathroom. I'll—" He stopped as the sound of shuffling footsteps reached them from upstairs.

From the shadows at the top of the stairs, an old man appeared. Gray-haired, a heavy growth of stubble on his lower face that didn't disguise the way the right side of it drooped. He was slightly bent to one side, leaning on the cane in his left hand.

"Brody," the man said, his voice a deep rumble, the syllables slightly slurred. "Who's this you've brought home with you?"

Brody might be thirty-four years old and consider himself to be an elite operator, but he still cringed at coming in late and waking up his old man. "Sorry we woke you, Dad. This is Trinity. She's a…friend of mine," he said, not knowing what else to say to explain this odd situation.

Rather than respond, his father shuffled down the stairs, staring at her. Trinity didn't move, watching his father come toward them closely, without a word.

Brody hated that this was how she was seeing him for the first time. Back in the day, his father had been one of the most feared and respected gunny sergeants the Corps had ever produced. Before the stroke that had crippled him two years ago, he'd still been as strong and fit as most men half his age. It would always hurt him to see his dad this way, withered and partially paralyzed, the right side of his mouth and eye drooping.

But there was nothing withered about his father's brain.

Those sharp hazel eyes moved from Trinity and back to him as his dad stopped on the bottom stair. Just high enough so that Brody had to look up at him a bit. Still the unmistakable master of this house, and the land it stood on. "Your *friend's* hurt," his father said, the pointed statement blade-sharp despite his slurred speech.

Brody resisted the urge to rub the back of his neck and lower his gaze. His old man was a formidable son of a bitch, even now. "She's a friend of my commander and his wife. She needed a place to stay for the night, so I brought her here."

His father turned his intense gaze on Trinity, who still hadn't moved. "What happened to you?" he asked her bluntly.

To her credit, Trinity stepped forward and offered her hand. Her left hand, since she'd noticed his father couldn't move his right arm. It touched something inside Brody, to see that gesture of unspoken respect. "I'm Trinity." She didn't stare and there was no discernable pity in her expression as she looked at him. Brody relaxed more.

"Gray Colebrook," his father replied, setting his cane aside to shake her hand. "So," he began as he took his cane up again. "What happened to you, young lady?"

"I had a car accident," she replied, and Brody had to admire her smooth, unruffled response. Not too many people could withstand the full effect of Grayson Colebrook's penetrating stare without being rattled to some extent, but she appeared completely at ease. "I appreciate you and your son letting me stay the night. I'll be on my way first thing in the morning."

His father grunted, clearly not convinced. "Not at all. And you're welcome to stay as long as you need," he added, taking Brody by surprise. Everyone knew his father didn't like company outside of family. Since the stroke, he'd become almost as much of a recluse as Wyatt. "Take her upstairs and put her in Charlie's old room," he said to Brody. "Then I want a word with you."

"Yes sir." He felt like he was fifteen all over again and busted for coming in after curfew as he ushered Trinity upstairs. "You can stay in here," he told her, opening the door to Charlie's room.

"Is Charlie your brother?"

"My sister, Charlotte. I've got two brothers as well." The eldest of whom, Wyatt, was no doubt alone right now in the cabin he lived in, a stone's throw from the main house. Miserable, solitary bastard that he'd become.

Brody gestured to the bathroom across the hall. "Go have a hot shower and get warm, you'll feel better. There are plenty of towels in the cupboard." Just the thought of what she'd look like standing beneath the water as it sluiced over her naked curves had his blood heating.

She stared up at him for a moment, and Brody once again felt himself being pulled under the spell of those hypnotic, deep blue eyes. He could all too easily imagine cupping that soft cheek in his hand as he leaned down to taste that tempting full lower lip. She radiated an air of absolute confidence and self-possession that he found irresistible, and coupled with her looks and that body in addition to her secret skill set that had him wanting to know all about her...

Yeah, it was probably best that she was only staying for one night. He was no stranger to women, and even though he suspected she was accustomed to using her looks to get what she wanted, there was no reason for her to play him. So he was pretty sure that the attraction simmering between them was mutual and that was as big a rush as taking out a target during a mission.

"Thanks," she murmured, her gaze lingering on his for a moment before she turned and closed the bedroom door behind her.

Feeling strangely protective of her, he went downstairs and found his father in the living room, ensconced in his favorite brown leather recliner, his feet propped up on the footrest and the cane within easy reach.

"Sit," his father said gruffly.

Brody sank onto the couch opposite him, wincing as his stiff left thigh twinged.

His father's gaze dipped to Brody's leg before moving up to meet his eyes. "You're looking better. Moving better."

"Yeah, I'm doing a lot better. Been working hard rebuilding the muscle mass I've got left. Stiffened up on me some during the drive. It'll be better in the morning." He rubbed at the sore muscles in his hip. That tackle by Trinity earlier hadn't helped matters. "Still not sure how things are gonna go down the road in terms of operational ability, but it's early days yet." He wasn't giving up hope that he'd still be able to rejoin his team at the end of all this. That was his goal, and he would do everything he could to make sure it happened.

"So. What happened to her?" his father asked.

"I don't really know," Brody admitted, keeping his voice down so Trinity couldn't hear him from upstairs. In a way he felt bad about telling his father Trinity's business when it was clear she didn't want anyone to know, but since he'd brought her here and she might pose a threat, his dad had a right to know. "Not sure if you remember me saying that my commander's wife has serious training."

"Yeah. And?"

"Apparently, Trinity's like her, but not a sniper." More of a femme fatale-type, if Brody guessed right. He could totally see why she'd be good at it. A couple hours in her company and he was already interested in her. Any man with a pulse would be.

His father's graying eyebrows drew together. "She's military?"

"No. I don't know what they are, but I'm pretty sure they're government agents of some kind."

"What kind of agents?"

"They're pros, Dad."

"Hitters?" he asked, the question sharp despite the slurred speech.

Now Brody rubbed the back of his neck, feeling uncomfortable under his old man's scrutiny. "I think so, yeah."

His father was quiet for a moment, leaning back in his chair to absorb that little nugget of info. "So, her accident. It wasn't an accident."

There was no way he was even going to try to sugar coat this; his father would see right through it and be pissed off. "She was on a job tonight. Someone targeted her afterward, ran her off the road. Her car crashed into a lake and she managed to swim out, find her way to my commander's place and shut down his home security system. That's how DeLuca knew something was up and asked me to swing by to check it out. I couldn't just leave her there."

"No," his father agreed. "But she's a target."

"Yeah. I figured she'd be as safe here as anywhere, and it's only for the night." Maybe. Unless he could convince her to stay until she was fully healed, or at least until she could put a solid plan together. "And if anything *did* happen, we could take care of it." We, as in he and Wyatt. A lethal combination, even considering Wyatt's injuries. Whoever was hunting Trinity would have to be insane to attack a place housing two former SOF Marines and a female assassin.

But Brody would be on guard for trouble, just in case it came looking.

His old man studied him in silence with those miss-nothing hazel eyes, that laser-like stare as potent as ever despite the way his right eye drooped. "You sure you know what you're doing?"

I sure as hell hope so. "I'm just doing a favor for my commander." That's what he told himself, even if he already felt involved and didn't want to see anything happen to Trinity. "She'll move on as soon as she's well enough."

They both looked up as the guest bathroom door opened and her hushed footsteps crossed the floor above their heads. Charlie's door shut a moment later.

Glancing back at him, his father gave a decisive nod. "She'll be safe as long as she's here. But you watch your back," he added in the way only a man who'd served multiple combat deployments and seen death and destruction up close and personal could.

"I will." Relieved that his father was on board with the plan, he stood, mentally cursing the way the muscles in his left leg and hip threatened to give out. "'Night,

Dad."

"Sleep tight, Son. It's good to have you home."

"Thanks. It's good to be home." He'd needed this time so badly.

Brody settled himself in the bedroom he used to share with Wyatt when they were growing up, but even when he was under the quilt on the new queen-size bed, he couldn't sleep.

He was too busy thinking about the captivating, sexy woman sleeping in the next room.

Chapter FIVE

B rody was up early the next morning, dressed and creeping down the wooden stairs toward the kitchen by five. He'd been worried he'd sleep in and miss hearing Trinity stirring but when he'd passed her room just now the door was still closed.

Unless she'd slipped out of the house while he was asleep.

Frowning, he stopped in the middle of the stairs. Could she have snuck out without him noticing? It seemed ridiculous, but Trinity wasn't exactly an average woman.

He crept back up the stairs and stood outside her door, listening intently. When there was no movement he thought about cracking her door open to steal a peek but if she was still in bed that would surely wake her. And let's face it, if she was gone there was nothing he could do about it anyway. He'd find out either way soon enough.

As he headed down to the kitchen, he was surprised

to realize how much he'd been looking forward to seeing her this morning. He'd thought about her a lot last night, wondering who she was, who she worked for, and why she'd become an assassin. She'd certainly made one hell of an impression, and he'd be lying if he said he didn't want her.

After turning on the coffee pot he dug out his cell phone. Both Briar and DeLuca had asked for an update about Trinity. He'd just started to type out a response when the back door opened.

Wyatt strode in, the slightly altered rhythm of his steps unmistakable on the old plank floors. He stopped when he saw Brody standing there. "Hey. Saw your truck out front. When did you get in?"

His big brother was older than him by sixteen months and an inch taller, had the same solid build as him and Easton. The scarring on the right side of his face looked a lot better than it had at the start of his recovery, and the glass eye they'd given him looked real. His prosthetic lower leg was hidden by his jeans, and due to months of therapy following the amputation, his gait was smoother than Brody's was now. But on the inside, Wyatt was permanently damaged by what had happened to him in Afghanistan.

"Got in late last night." Growing up, they'd been really close, especially after their mom died. Since being wounded, Wyatt had pushed him and everyone else away. Brody had given him the space he'd wanted, but he missed his big brother like hell, and the relationship they'd had for so long. He kept hoping that one day things would change back to the way they had been.

A soft scratching sounded at the door. Wyatt shot an annoyed glance at it then pushed it open. A moment later a small brown and white spaniel trotted inside, its long ears flopping with each step and its feathery white tail swishing back and forth in a blur.

Brody's eyebrows went up. Wyatt loved animals more than anybody Brody knew, yet he'd flat out refused to get a dog since being injured. "Who's this?"

"Grits," Wyatt muttered, sounding annoyed.

"Grits? As in, shrimp and grits?" At the mention of its name, the dog stopped and stretched its neck out to sniff at Brody's pant leg, its large brown eyes gazing up at him with a melting expression. Brody reached down to scratch its soft head and the dog flinched, backed away.

"He's a little skittish of strangers," Wyatt said.

Brody straightened, giving the dog space to get used to him. "What the hell kind of name is that for a dog?"

Wyatt made a face and reached into the cupboard for a mug. "Beats the hell outta me."

"Is he yours?"

"For the time being, yeah."

He didn't sound too happy about it and Brody wasn't surprised. Wyatt had owned only shepherds or Malinois. Big, strong working dogs, the kinds he'd worked with back in his days in the Corps, up until he'd been wounded. His military dog, Raider, had been killed in the same blast that cost Wyatt his leg and eye. He'd never recovered from the loss, had sworn he'd never own another dog. It was almost as though he didn't trust himself with one again, or maybe it was some kind of self-punishment.

And yet…here was Grits.

When Brody kept watching him without saying anything else, Wyatt sighed and leaned against the counter, folding his arms across his chest. "Piper brought him over a couple weeks ago, said he needed a foster home. Found him through some rescue organization."

Didn't take a genius to figure out that Piper was hoping the dog would tug on whatever heartstrings

Wyatt had left, so he wouldn't be able to give the dog up. "Really." Ballsy move by Wyatt's former high school girlfriend, to just bring the dog over without asking, but Brody loved that about her.

Though she and Wyatt had broken up when he'd left for boot camp, they'd always stayed in touch. Piper was married now and although neither one of them carried a torch for the other anymore, she had stayed close with the family and still came over to visit their dad and give Wyatt a kick in the ass when he needed one. Which was pretty often. She was a sweetheart with a backbone of steel, and an adored honorary member of the family.

"Said she thought he'd be good company for me." Wyatt sounded like the words left a bad taste in his mouth.

Yeah, Brody bet that had gone over well. "He's pretty cute." He held out his hand for the dog to sniff it. When Grits inched forward, head lowered and tail wagging, he slowly reached down to scratch his soft little white chin and got a series of lightning fast puppy kisses on his hand for his effort. "Seems like he's got a nice personality."

Wyatt just grunted and filled his coffee mug, but Brody could sense the grudging affection he had for the little guy, and the truth was, if Wyatt truly didn't want Grits, he'd have found another home for him already. Wyatt might be a gruff, grim bastard these days, but he had a giant soft spot for animals and damsels in distress.

Speaking of damsels... Brody's gaze strayed to the stairs, looking for Trinity.

"You want one?" Wyatt asked, coffee pot in hand.

"Yeah." God knew he needed the caffeine. He accepted the mug Wyatt handed him and they both stood there sipping at their coffee in a silence that quickly began to grate on his nerves.

They hadn't seen each other since Brody's fourth round of surgery seven weeks ago. He couldn't help but feel awkward, standing there on two functional legs while his brother had only one. Wyatt had never made it seem like he resented Brody for it, but Brody went out of his way not to rub his good fortune in his brother's face whenever they saw each other.

"So, you working on a house right now?" Brody asked.

"Not at the moment. Just sold off two mares and three others foaled recently, so it's been busy around here."

The horse farm operation he and their father ran wasn't as big as it had been prior to his dad's stroke, but it was big enough, paid the bills and kept him and Wyatt busy, along with the veterans Wyatt hired on as extra help. "What about the Miller place? Any word on it yet?" The Queen Anne-style Victorian home that had belonged to the grandmother of one of Wyatt's fallen friends was on the outskirts of town. He'd had his eye on it since the day the elderly Mrs. Miller had passed on, but so far her estate refused to sell it.

"No, and it's getting more run down every month. I hate seeing it like that. It's already been vacant going on three years. It needed plenty of repairs and updating back then. I can only imagine the state of the inside now." He shook his head. "Leaving that place vacant and letting it fall apart on that lot is a damn crime."

"They'll sell it sooner or later."

Wyatt scowled and swallowed a mouthful of coffee. "Not soon enough."

Relief flashed through Brody when he heard soft footsteps moving overhead a moment later, because it dissolved the subtle tension between him and Wyatt, but more because it confirmed that Trinity was still here.

Wyatt frowned and looked up at the ceiling. "Who

else is here?"

"I…brought someone with me," he said, not wanting to get into the details with Wyatt right now. Mostly since it was impossible to put into words why he'd actually brought her home with him.

Before his brother could say anything else, Trinity came into view on the stairs. Her sleek, black bob was mussed and she was moving way slower than she had last night. This morning she was dressed in a cherry-red sweater that hugged the ample curves of her breasts to perfection and the same snug jeans she'd had on last night. Her body screamed pinup model and her curves were sexy as hell.

She paused for a second when she saw them both standing there watching her, then resumed her course. "Morning," she murmured, her voice holding a sleepy huskiness that made Brody think of sex.

Slow, lazy, morning sex, the kind that left both partners totally sated and sliding back into sleep afterward. With her delectable body draped over his.

He shoved the image out of his head before his jeans got tight and glanced at Wyatt. His brother was frozen, his mug partway to his mouth, his gaze locked on Trinity with interest.

"Morning," Brody answered. "Get any sleep?"

"A little." She stepped into the light and he winced when he saw her face.

"Oh, wow. That's quite a shiner."

Her lips quirked in a quick, wry grin. "Yeah. I can feel the glow, let me tell you."

The dog ran up to her and jumped up to rest his paws on her knee, tail wagging like mad.

"Grits, *down*," Wyatt commanded sharply. The dog glanced back at him, ears perked, tail swishing back and forth, but didn't obey.

"It's okay." Trinity smiled at the dog then bent a

little, her movement stiff and slow as she leaned over to pet him. "He's cute."

"Yeah," Wyatt muttered in a sour tone, giving Grits a censuring look.

"I thought you said he was shy of strangers?" Brody asked him.

"He is. Usually."

Well he sure seemed to like Trinity well enough. Not that Brody could blame him. There was something about her that drew him like a magnet.

When she straightened she lifted a hand, grimaced as she rubbed at her neck and the top of her shoulder.

Brody winced in sympathy. She looked damn sore, a bruise spreading down her temple to her cheek and forming around her eye in shades of blue and purple. He still thought she was gorgeous, that innate poise radiating from her crazy attractive. "Here, let me get you some ice." He started for the fridge.

"No, it's okay—"

"You need ice. And an anti-inflammatory."

"Already took three." Coming to the bottom of the stairs, she stopped and looked at Wyatt questioningly, Grits at her feet. Again there was no shock in her expression, no pity as she stared at his brother and his scars. But maybe she was just one hell of an actress.

"This is my older brother, Wyatt," Brody said. "Wyatt, Trinity."

"Nice to meet you," Wyatt said with a nod, then shot him a questioning look and subtly raised an eyebrow. Brody wasn't going to explain everything with her standing right there though.

"Likewise," she answered.

"You want coffee?" Wyatt asked her.

"Please." Another smile, this one her easiest yet, and Brody felt a surprising, sharp prick of jealousy that she'd smiled at his brother that way instead of him.

Even though it felt like she'd been run over by a truck last night, Trinity managed a smile for Wyatt as he handed her a mug of coffee. Her head pounded and her neck and shoulders were on fire. The left side of her ribcage was tender and the side of her face was swollen.

It was nothing compared to what he must have gone through after his injuries.

"Thanks," she told him, covering a wince as she bent down to scratch the dog's ears again. She got a flurry of kisses for her trouble. Cute little fella.

Wyatt grunted in response and stepped back to lean against the counter, avoiding looking at her. The scarring on the right side of his face was pretty bad. The pockmarks and swirling patterns told her he'd suffered some kind of blast injury.

But she was more aware of the way Brody was watching her, and annoyed that she even cared. He was far too sexy standing there in worn jeans and a T-shirt that stretched across his sculpted chest.

There was tension between the brothers. It was subtle, but for someone like her who'd been trained at an early age to pick up on emotional cues, she'd noticed it the moment she'd seen them from the stairs. And she was pretty sure it had nothing to do with her showing up just now.

The silence continued to expand as they sipped their coffee and she had no interest in making things more uncomfortable for everyone by overstaying her welcome. Brody had done her a huge favor by bringing her here despite the potential risk to him and his family. She owed him, and the best way to repay him was to leave immediately. No matter the risk, she had to get back to D.C., retrieve her documents from her rental apartment and get her butt back to London.

Also, she didn't socialize much unless she was on a

job, so she wasn't used to hanging out with people outside of work. The idea of making small talk right now was simply too exhausting to think about.

She set her half-empty cup on the counter. "Well, I should probably get—"

The back door opened and Colebrook Senior appeared with a gray-muzzled basset hound waddling after him. He shuffled into the kitchen leaning on his cane, glanced between the three of them. "Any coffee left?" His gaze settled on her, and she had the disconcerting feeling that he was seeing into her mind. "You don't look so good."

Trinity blinked, stifled a laugh at the blunt assessment. "I've felt better."

"Get any sleep last night?"

"A little." Not nearly enough and it was going to catch up with her soon, which was why she needed to get moving. She hadn't slept more than a few snatches here and there, the ingrained need to be vigilant overriding her exhaustion. She'd come down as soon as she'd heard people moving around downstairs.

He jerked his chin at the staircase behind her. "Go have a hot shower and then climb back into bed."

The order didn't offend her. And while she appreciated his concern, she couldn't stay. "Thanks for your hospitality, but I should get going."

Brody frowned at her. "You're in no shape to go anywhere."

His tone made her bristle. "I'll be okay."

"He's right," Senior said, shuffling over to take the mug Wyatt offered him, then pinned her with a hard stare. "You're not leaving until I'm satisfied that you're well enough to go out on your own."

He leaned back against the counter and set his cane aside, adopting the exact same pose as his sons. It was downright eerie, how much their mannerisms were alike.

"I may be an old fart and look and sound like that guy from *Legends of the Fall*, but I was a Marine for a long time and I know when something doesn't feel right."

Trinity opened her mouth to downplay his concern but he cut her off with a shake of his head.

"If you're in trouble, then this is as safe a place as any for you."

"Trouble?" Wyatt asked, aiming a frown at her.

Senior tossed him a quelling look then focused back on her. "My sons and I can definitely watch out for you until you're better."

Her cheeks heated. It wasn't often that someone saw through her like that, let alone call her on her bullshit, but she still had to fight the urge to tell him she was every bit as well trained as they were. Brody must have told him about last night. He and his sons had been nothing but kind to her though and she knew he was just trying to help.

"I really should go," she said instead. All her instincts told her to leave and keep moving. It was what she'd been trained to do.

"Give it another day or two," Brody said, causing her to look over at him. Those dark eyes held hers and again she felt that deep, magnetic pull deep in her belly.

Another day or two might not seem like much to someone else, but in her world it was an eternity. He didn't know what she'd done or what she was up against. Who she was up against.

Tino's network had a long reach. They'd be watching airports and bus stations, train stations. She still doubted anyone would have been able to track her here, but she couldn't rule out that possibility entirely. She didn't want to put Brody or his family in any further danger by staying.

"Wyatt," Senior said abruptly as she and Brody kept staring at each other. "I need a hand with something outside."

Wyatt frowned at him but lowered his coffee cup into the sink and pushed away from the counter.

"Let's go, Sarge," Senior said to the basset hound, who groaned and got to his feet, waddling after his master on his short little legs.

Wyatt gave her one last curious glance before heading out the door behind his father. "Grits. Come." Grits scrambled after him, toenails clicking on the wooden floor, and disappeared out the door with a happy swish of his tail.

In the silence that followed Brody set his cup down and crossed to her. She had the strongest urge to back away, but held her ground. He stopped a foot away, close enough for her to smell the scent of soap and coffee, and for her to feel herself getting lost in his dark brown eyes.

Not good.

"You need more recovery time," he said softly, his deep voice like an intimate caress. "Not to mention food and sleep. I may not know you, but even I can tell you're nowhere near the top of your game right now. Give it another day or two. Do you even have a plan figured out yet?"

"Yes." Of course she had a damn plan. She hadn't lived this long, doing what she did, without being able to improvise and adapt quickly to whatever happened.

The growing attraction between them felt strange and she immediately tried to quell her response because she didn't trust it. Even if she was open to a mutually satisfying fling, it wasn't going to be with someone so closely tied to Matt and Briar. That just felt too awkward and personal. She liked to keep her private life secret, and well removed from every other aspect of her life. It was the only part of her life that was truly hers, and she guarded it fiercely.

"There are people after me. I don't want to put you or your family at further risk. You've done more than enough for me already, now it's time for me to move on."

Rather than answer he lifted a hand, reached up as though he was going to touch her face.

Trinity held her breath as he gently eased the hair away from the side of her face. His fingertips brushed her cheek, light as a sigh, yet she felt it all over. Her nipples tightened against her bra and a burst of arousal sparked in her belly. She had the strongest urge to lean forward and cover his lips with hers, slowly savor the taste of him.

Shocked by how much she was tempted to initiate something she knew she shouldn't, she stepped back, needing distance between them. What the hell was wrong with her? She never let her guard down, never let her personal needs get in the way. She was literally on the run, in hiding, and should be one hundred percent focused on how she was going to get back to D.C. and out of the country undetected, not letting herself get sidetracked by physical desire.

Brody lowered his hand, his gaze still locked with hers, filled with heated awareness that made her pulse trip. "Don't worry about any of that right now. Go take that shower and then get some sleep. If trouble shows up here, believe me, we can handle it."

She shook her head, winced as her sore muscles grabbed. "I don't want you to have to do that." It wasn't right. Brody was recovering from whatever had injured him, and his brother and father were going through their own hardships. They'd all been through too much already. She refused to add more to their burden.

"I know, but if you leave now in this condition, you'll be even more at risk."

He was right. Much as she hated to admit it, she

was nowhere near ready to attempt to go back to D.C. and the threat waiting for her there. Without her documents, fake ID and credit cards, there was no way she was getting out of the country.

"Give it another day or two," he said again, and gave her a little smile. "For me."

She frowned at the last part. "Why would I do that?"

He nodded. "Because now I'm involved, and I don't want to see anything happen to you."

That made no sense, because he didn't even know her, but it had sounded sincere. She didn't know what to say.

With that he headed outside, leaving her staring after him with an unsettling and powerful sense of longing unfurling inside her.

Chapter SIX

After a long, hot shower Trinity dressed and stepped out of the bathroom with a clearer head and almost groaned at the smell of bacon frying downstairs. She entered the kitchen and found Brody at the stove with his back to her, a tea towel draped over one broad shoulder.

For just a moment she let her gaze travel up and down the length of him, let herself wonder what it would be like to sleep with him. Not that she'd ever indulge in that kind of fantasy, especially not while on the run, but still, the man had awoken something inside her, made her feel things that she hadn't felt in a long time.

It felt…magical to know she was still capable of it, even though she knew she had to suppress the urge.

Brody looked over his shoulder at her, his lips curving in a welcoming smile that set off a series of flutters in the pit of her stomach. God, her body was suddenly acting like a crushed-out teenager around him. "Hungry?"

"Starved." Still sore but the shower and painkillers had helped. The urge to keep moving was strong, rooted in her from years of some of the toughest training on the planet, but Brody and his father were right; she needed more time to recover before heading out on her own. She was just grateful they were willing to let her stay under the circumstances. They were special people, to step up and help her at a time like this.

She moved closer to the stove. Brody was frying up the bacon and there was already a pile of pancakes waiting on a plate next to him. Her stomach growled and her mouth watered. "I haven't eaten bacon in forever," she said, eyeing the sizzling strips in the pan longingly. All that salty, smoky, greasy awesomeness.

"I don't eat it much either, but it was in the fridge, so…"

The farmhouse-style table only had two settings on it. The idea of sharing a meal with him, alone, felt incredibly intimate. "Are your dad and brother not joining us?"

"Nah, they said they're doing some work on the fences and won't be back for a few hours. I think they're giving us some privacy."

She frowned. "Why?"

He gave her a heated look that clearly said he was aware of the chemistry between them, maybe even open to exploring it, and it shocked her how much the idea appealed to her. "Savor the peace and quiet while you can. I'm way better company than those two grumpy-assed recluses anyhow."

Seemed to her they had their reasons for being grumpy recluses, but she kept that to herself and glanced around the great room that connected the kitchen and family room. A group of framed pictures on the mantel above the fireplace in the family room caught her eye.

She headed over to them, curious about Brody and

his family, again struck by how odd this situation was. Here she was, in his inner sanctum, surrounded by his family's keepsakes and memories when he knew next to nothing about her. Kind of unfair.

It didn't stop her from studying the pictures, however.

She recognized Brody immediately, and there was a shot of Wyatt in his combat utilities before his injury. One recent family portrait showed all four siblings—the three boys and their sister, Charlie—together with their dad. All were brown-haired. Brody, the younger brother and Charlie all had brown eyes, and Wyatt and Colebrook senior had hazel. Every one of them was fit, the men muscular, and one look told her they'd all served in the military. Maybe even Charlie.

From out of nowhere an unexpected, sharp pang hit her at seeing the picture of their happy family unit. A little envy maybe, but more than that, a longing for something she'd always secretly wanted and never had. Would probably never be able to have, after the life she'd led.

"Your other brother," she called out to him. "Is he still in the Marine Corps?"

"Easton," Brody answered without turning around. "And no, he's got a government job now."

His ambiguous answer wasn't a surprise. Brody didn't know her, didn't owe her any answers, but whatever job Easton had, she'd bet it wasn't a desk job.

Trinity perused the other pictures, lingering on another one of the four siblings, this time the others gathered around Wyatt in his hospital bed soon after he'd been wounded, him grinning through the bandages covering his head and right side of his face.

That image told her everything she needed to know about the Colebrooks. They looked after their own and stood by each other, through good times and bad, no matter what. And it seemed they'd been there to support Wyatt through what must have been the hardest time in his life. Her respect for them just kept growing. Not everyone was lucky enough to have that sort of support network.

The only picture of the mother was a family portrait taken maybe twenty years ago or so if Trinity judged the hairstyles and clothing correctly, when Brody and his siblings were young. Maybe elementary school age or slightly older.

She wasn't going to ask what had happened to her, since it was pretty clear that she was now out of the picture, for whatever reason. Given what she already knew of the family, it seemed reasonable to surmise that she'd probably passed away.

It made her heart ache for Brody and his siblings. They were obviously a tight-knit, loving family. Losing a parent was never easy, but when it happened to young children, it changed everything, forever. She knew that better than anyone.

A pang of wistfulness hit her as she remembered something she didn't want to dwell on right now. Or ever.

Feeling like she knew the Colebrooks a little better already, Trinity wandered back into the kitchen while Brody finished up the bacon. She fought the urge to fidget, the cynical part of her disliking that he was doing this for her. In her experience when someone did something for her, they almost always wanted something in return. Especially a man.

Nothing was ever given for free. And it drove her nuts to be hiding here in this beautiful family's home when there were people out there hunting her. Today she had to do some research, put some feelers out and find out what Tino had been up to since last night. When she left this place, she needed every advantage she could get.

"Can I help with anything?" she asked.

"Yeah, you can go sit and drink your juice while I finish up."

Still not trusting his motives completely, she went to the table and took a seat, watching him work at the stove. Each time he moved, the muscles in his back and arms flexed. She imagined sliding her hands beneath his shirt, smoothing her palms over his bare skin to map each ridge and hollow. Stroking. Teasing.

What would it hurt? a little voice whispered inside her. *You'll be gone soon enough and you'll never see him again anyway. Why not indulge this once?*

Brody set a loaded plate in front of her then rounded the table to sit opposite her with his own. "Dig in."

She picked up a piece of bacon, fighting a smile.

"What?" he asked with a grin.

"Never had a guy cook for me before."

His eyebrows rose, his fork paused partway to his mouth with a wedge of syrup-drenched pancake stuck to it. "Ever?"

She nodded and bit into the bacon, moaned a little at the salty, smoky flavor. "Oh my God…" She tended to gain weight easily and her job required her to keep her shape. Eating bacon and pancakes for breakfast felt deliciously sinful.

He chuckled, the deep sound making her think naughty things. "I don't know what kind of guys you usually date, but you need to raise your bar a little."

She lowered her gaze to her plate and didn't answer. She didn't date, hadn't in years. Her job wouldn't allow it, and she'd never met anyone she'd trusted enough to want a relationship with anyway.

A man like Brody, though, with his security clearance and job as part of the FBI's most elite hostage rescue and counter terrorism team… Yeah, he tempted her in ways she'd never been tempted before.

Adding to that, he was a damn good cook. The bacon was perfect, no soggy bits and not overdone, the pancakes light and fluffy. She narrowed her eyes at him in suspicion. "You made these from scratch, or from a box?"

His eyes gleamed with amusement as he looked across the table at her. "Scratch."

He was serious. "Who taught you to cook?"

"My dad. My mom passed away when we were young. Cancer."

"I'm sorry," she murmured. "That must have been hard."

"Yeah, thanks. It was tough on all of us, but my old man was tougher. He raised us all on his own after that, did the best he could."

"I think you turned out all right." Better than all right.

He shrugged those wide shoulders. "I like to think so. What about you? You close to your parents?"

She scooped up a forkful of pancake. "No, I never knew them. My mother left me at an orphanage when I was still a baby." She wasn't sure why she'd told him that. Maybe because it was only fair after what she'd already learned about him.

"Oh. So you're adopted?"

She shook her head, gave a rueful smile to hide that deep ache she'd always felt at never being wanted. "Nope. I was in the foster system for a while after that but nothing ever worked out." And then she'd been recruited into the Valkyrie program and her life had changed forever.

They finished eating in companionable silence, with Trinity aware of everything about him. It was impossible to ignore the man's sheer presence, and eating alone with him like this had all her attention attuned to him.

"How's your head?" he asked her.

"Still holding together, thanks." She'd been careful when she'd washed her hair not to disturb the adhesive.

The crunch of footsteps on gravel made her glance toward the back door and then Colebrook Senior appeared there, Sarge at his heels. He had a rolled up newspaper in one hand.

Brody stood up as if to go help him but his father waved him off with an irritated expression and clomped over to the table. The way his gaze held hers set off warning bells and made her stomach muscles grab.

"Something you might want to see," he said, and set the paper down in front of her.

She read the headline while Brody leaned over to look at it. *Wealthy D.C. Magnate Murdered.*

Cold spread through her gut as she scanned the story.

The writer reported that Franco Salvatori had been stabbed in the neck with a highly lethal dose of toxin, and his bodyguard reported it had been Eva Gregorivich, the woman Salvatori had been with last night at a local gala. The cops had pulled the car she was reported to have stolen from a lake with the back window shot out. It showed a picture of Eva at a previous function and finished with the police asking for the public's help in locating her.

Trinity blanched. She'd thought Tino would want to keep this on the down low, since Salvatori had died on his watch. He must be desperate to flush her out if he'd gone to the cops, and she knew damn well he'd likely reached out to a detective he had in his pocket.

"That you?" Senior asked her, indicating the photo of Eva.

She was an expert liar, could lie her way out of damn near anything, but looking into those sharp hazel eyes, she just couldn't. God, she should never have come here, regretted ever getting into Brody's truck last night. "Yes," she murmured.

A beat of taut silence passed as the older man studied her. "I don't know what's going on or who you work for, but it looks like you've got a serious problem here."

She pushed to her feet, ignoring the stab of pain in her head, her only thought leaving this place and this family before she brought any harm to them.

"Wait," Brody said but she ignored him and rushed up the stairs, intent on grabbing the bag she'd packed that held her pistol, extra ammo and a change of clothes.

When she turned around Brody was standing inside the door. She froze, lifted her chin, her heart beating faster at the set look on his face. "I can't stay here."

"Yes you can." He shut the door and advanced on her. "He wasn't telling you so you'd leave, he was telling you to warn you."

She backed up a step, and her spine came up against the wall. Her heart hammered against her ribs as he crowded her personal space, not stopping until he stood inches from her.

With slow deliberation he lifted his hands and placed them on either side of her head, caging her in, his eyes on hers. And just like that, her body cried out for him, aching for his touch, the feel of his mouth on hers.

"You might not trust anyone, but you're on my turf now. Nobody puts my family in danger, so cut the bullshit and tell me exactly what's going on." He paused a beat, his eyes searching hers. "Who do you work for?"

It wouldn't cost her anything to tell him that much. "I was hired as a contract agent for the hit by a government agency."

"Which agency?" His voice was hard, authoritative.

"I can't tell you that."

He didn't say anything for a moment. "Why did

they want Salvatori dead?"

"Because he was an evil piece of shit doing illegal arms trades and sex trafficking. And because he was putting undercover agents at risk by selling information to the enemy here." Sleeper cell members who would love nothing more than to unleash hell on American soil.

"What's a Valkyrie?"

No way she was answering that. Time was ticking. She'd told him enough, wanted to stop him from asking any more questions. He was so close, the heat from his body sank into hers...

Desire burned in his gaze along with the anger. A desire she could use to her advantage, though that seemed distasteful now.

Trinity set her hands on his shoulders. Those hard, warm muscles bunched beneath her palms, setting off a burst of heat inside her. She looked down at his mouth, deliberately parted her lips in a practiced move designed to draw his attention there.

His dark gaze heated, dipped to her mouth. A tendril of longing spread through her belly. The urge to thread her hands into his dark hair and kiss him was intense; the need to distract him even stronger. Brody hadn't moved, but she could feel the silent tension thrumming inside him, the desire he couldn't hide.

With her back still touching the wall she leaned her head forward to brush her lips over his. He stiffened for a moment but didn't pull away, his breath warm on her face.

He was a challenge she couldn't resist.

That he didn't give in right away, that he was making her wait, made this even hotter. She didn't understand the attraction between them and certainly didn't trust it, but it was there whether she wanted it to be or not. She allowed her eyes to drift close, her body to sway more fully against his as she opened her lips under his.

To her surprise, Brody wrenched his head back. Her eyes flew open and his dark gaze hardened with anger. "I'm not a mark for you to seduce. Don't play with me."

For a moment Trinity was too shocked to respond. She was so used to men turning into putty in her hand. When she turned on the seductress routine and made a move, none of them ever stood a chance. Yet Brody had seen right through it. Granted, she looked like hell right now, but God, maybe she really was losing her appeal.

He felt good pressed up against her like this. Edgy, a little dangerous even, but not in a threatening way. He would never hurt her physically. He wasn't built that way.

He released her and stepped back, but it was clear from the heated look he gave her that things weren't finished between them, and that scared the hell out of her.

Let's see him walk away from this.

Pride stinging, not about to let him have the last word, she grabbed his head and fused her mouth to his, putting her entire body into this kiss.

Brody knew exactly what she was doing.

He'd pissed her off by calling her out on the attempt to distract him and she wanted to get back at him. Wanted to prove she still had the upper hand in this, but he'd be damned if he'd give in, no matter how good the kiss was.

He refused to let her win this battle of wills, didn't matter how much he wanted her or how much she made his head spin. She seduced men for a living and wouldn't respect him unless he proved a worthy adversary. He hated that, hated that she sold her body that way. It was just damn hard to remember all that when all he wanted to do was lose himself in her.

Instead he slowed things down, seizing control of the kiss.

Sliding one hand into her hair to cradle the back of her head, he brought the other up to cup the uninjured side of her face. Her eyes flew open and he caught the flare of surprise there before he closed his and sank into the kiss.

He held her head in a firm but careful grip and stroked his tongue against hers gently, teasing, then withdrew to suck at her lower lip. She tasted sweet, like maple syrup.

Brody licked along her lower lip, a light graze of his tongue to make her crave more. A heady surge of triumph washed through him when she let out a tiny gasp and pushed closer yet, her fingers digging into his scalp in a clear demand for more.

Knowing he needed to leave her wanting more, or at least crack that impenetrable, cool mask she hid behind, he slowed the kiss even further. Soft, lazy movements of lips and tongue that made his heart pound and his already rigid cock ache. It was so goddamn erotic, hotter than the last sex he'd had, with someone whose name he couldn't even remember at the moment.

To his surprise Trinity made a quiet sound of yearning in the back of her throat and slowed to match his languid pace, her full, ripe curves seeming to melt into him. She was such an enigma. Composed and aloof one moment, then full of fire and passion the next.

He couldn't know for sure but something told him she'd been hurt by a man in the past, maybe even sexually. The idea made him furious but it also made him want to soothe and comfort her, to show her not all men were evil assholes bent on using their strength against her. She was used to using her body and sexual skill as a weapon but his gut said that initial burst of surprise from her was real. Another wave of lust blasted through him.

She was into this. Into him. And he had to be careful not to let her know how bad he wanted that.

But then his plan to turn the tables on her backfired.

The way she responded, the way her body molded to his made it impossible to think straight. The tiny catch in her breathing when he once again explored her mouth with his tongue had him itching to start peeling off her clothes so he could touch and taste her delicate skin. Build her need so high that she'd forget about the power struggle and surrender to the pleasure he was more than willing to give her.

Trinity made an impatient sound in the back of her throat and nipped at his lower lip but he resisted the challenge, keeping things slow and soft. He slid the hand in her hair down to cradle her nape, squeezed his fingers around the back of her neck.

She froze, a surprised moan of pleasure-pain spilling from her. Brody did it again, a little harder, and she pulled her mouth free, groaning in relief as he kneaded her sore, tight muscles. "Oh God," she whispered, leaning into his touch, her expression somewhere between pain and ecstasy.

Stifling a chuckle, he bent to feather kisses over the corner of her mouth. "Feel good?"

"God, yes. Don't stop…"

An entirely different image of her begging like that burst into his mind. He imagined them both naked. He was on top of her, sucking at one of her luscious breasts as he pumped his hips and drove his rock hard cock in and out of her slick heat. He almost groaned aloud, he wanted that so badly.

But not if she was giving in just to play him.

He raised his head, studied her face and squeezed with his fingers once more. She appeared to be seriously loving what he was doing. Her eyes were still closed and her head now resting back against the wall.

Knowing he was making her feel good and easing her pain filled him with tenderness. He moved his other hand from her face and down to the top of her shoulder, squeezed the taut edge of her upper trapezius muscle. A long, liquid moan of bliss escaped her.

This time he couldn't hold back a chuckle. "Come here," he murmured, drawing her close once more.

She went willingly, without an ounce of resistance. Brody cradled her head to his chest and kept massaging her sore muscles as he maneuvered them both backward to the queen-size bed behind him.

He stretched out on his side and drew her down next to him. When she didn't protest, just followed him down with her eyes still closed, he pulled her into his body and resumed the massage, starting at the top of her neck and working his way down to the middle of her back.

Her hands crept up his ribs, fingers flexing gently, exploring him. He wished they were both naked but it was probably better that they weren't because he didn't think he'd be able to stop until he was buried inside her. And the only way he was willing to let things go that far was if it was a mutual sharing of pleasure.

She nestled against him, burying her face in the curve of his shoulder, and his heart squeezed at the gesture. "Too hard?" he murmured into her hair.

"No. Perfect," she mumbled, then made a soft humming noise that drove him nuts. There was no way she could miss the feel of his erection shoved against her but she didn't seem to mind and she felt so goddamn good cuddled up to him like this…

Brody closed his eyes and kept up the rhythmic motion of his hands, digging his fingers into the places that made her moan and wriggle against him. It was torture, but the best kind and he was in no hurry to see it end. The back door opened and shut downstairs—his dad was giving them more time alone in the house.

He didn't know how long they spent that way while he rubbed and squeezed her tight muscles, giving extra attention and pressure where she needed it most, imagining the sounds she'd make for him if he rolled her to her back, peeled her jeans off and buried his mouth between her legs.

He sucked in a steadying breath, fought to banish the fantasy of her stretched out beneath him, naked, her legs wrapped around his neck and those elegant hands digging into his bare shoulders as she writhed beneath the stroke of his tongue and begged him for more.

As the minutes passed she grew more pliant, leaning more of her weight into him. She quieted, her breathing turning slow and even in the quiet room.

He gentled his movements, simply smoothing his hands up and down her back, hard as hell and dying for more yet strangely content to hold her this way. She gave a tiny twitch and that was when he realized she was asleep.

He stilled his hands on her back, the warmth of her sinking into his palms and chest. He might not know her very well but he knew that someone with her training and background wouldn't fall asleep in his arms unless she trusted him on a subconscious level. The knowledge humbled him and caused a strange tightening in his chest.

He'd set out to teach her a lesson, give her a taste of her own medicine.

Instead he'd wound up falling deeper under her spell.

Chapter SEVEN

Tino cut the wires on the last security camera mounted on this side of the building's exterior and climbed down the ladder. This entire job was a pain in the ass but it had to be done. He'd called in a lot of favors just to get this far—just to find the place where his CIA contact thought Trinity might have been staying prior to killing Salvatori.

The moment Salvatori's death had hit the media airwaves, Tino could feel the invisible noose tightening around his throat. More and more people in his network were finding out what had happened, and they all knew he had been assigned as Salvatori's head of security.

His rep was in tatters. He'd been up all night trying to get a lead on Eva Gregorivich... Or at least find out who she really was and who she worked for.

Now he finally had a name.

Trinity Durant. Worked as a contractor for various government agencies. This time, it was the CIA. Or at least, he was pretty sure about that.

Salvatori's boss had tasked him with finding out who was gunning for them. He wasn't dropping the ball on this one. More than restoring his rep, this was about survival. If the Big Boss didn't get what he wanted, he might order a hit on Tino. And as good as he was, he didn't stand a chance against all the Mob's resources. He couldn't run, not without being found, and he didn't have the money to start a new life in some country overseas anyway.

He slipped the wire cutters back into his tool belt. Didn't matter if anyone in the building saw him. The security company uniform gave him the perfect excuse to be here and allowed him the freedom to move around in plain view.

It was the potential eyes watching him from the shadows that concerned him.

He could feel them out there. Someone was watching him and he was betting it was someone sent here on direct orders from the Big Boss. It made the back of his neck prickle.

Impatient to get answers, Tino headed up to apartment 4C. The solid brick building on the outskirts of D.C. had been built in the late 1800s and renovated with significant upgrades a few years ago, including a security system for both the building and each apartment.

The new-looking carpet along the hallway silenced his steps as he walked to 4C. At the door he paused to check for anti-tampering devices. If this Durant woman was a pro used by government agencies, then he wouldn't put it past her to set up some tricks like that.

Using a few tools from his kit, he jimmied the lock open and turned the knob. Easing the door open a few inches, he waited, but nothing tripped his internal radar. He stepped inside, shut the door and immediately got to work disabling the alarm system.

Once that was done he scanned the apartment. *Not a bad place to call home while you're on a job.* He sneered as he took in the shiny wood floors and granite countertops in the kitchen.

Within a few moments of searching around though, something was off. There were no hints or indications of any kind that anybody had been staying here. No coats or shoes in the hall closet. No dishes in the sink or dishwasher. No food in the fridge. Nothing left out on any of the tables.

He headed to the bedroom, his pulse beating faster. The bed was untouched, perfectly made. Again, there was nothing in the closets. He stalked into the bathroom. Empty. Not even a bar of soap in the shower. Nothing in the trash can. Had she even freaking *been* here?

A mix of frustration and anxiety churned in his stomach as he pulled out his phone and dialed his CIA contact. "It's me," he said, fighting back his annoyance. He'd used up all his leverage with this contact to get this location, and now he wondered if he was in the wrong damn place. "I'm at the apartment. There's nothing here. Literally, nothing." He rushed back out to the bedroom and began searching through the drawers in the bedside table and dresser. Empty.

Dammit. He could lift some prints or search for a hair sample for DNA testing in order to verify that she'd been here, but he might not get anything and it did jack for him at this point because he didn't have the time to wait around. He needed answers *now*. "Are you sure she was here?"

The man gave an irritated snort. "I'm sure. That's all I can say. She was staying there up until last night. I don't know for how long though. Maybe a week."

If she had, it did little good for him now. "And you're sure she was working alone? There's no one else she would have called for backup?"

"My source was clear about her working alone for this job, on a contract basis."

Tino didn't dare ask him who the source was, or what agency he worked for. He'd pushed the limits of this connection already. Even if his inside guy was lying, there was no way to know for sure at the moment. "Yeah. Thanks," he muttered, and hung up. "For nothing."

Standing there in the middle of the bedroom, he ran a gloved hand through his hair. He'd been so sure he'd find something here. Some clue that would help him track her down, because he didn't see any way she would have been able to get here and clear it out before skipping town.

He didn't think she would have risked coming here last night and wiping the place down, not with her injury—she had to be injured from the car wreck at least. So there should have been something here for him to find. Had the FBI or CIA or whatever come in and done a clean sweep last night? To erase any possible threads connecting her with them, and to Salvatori's death?

Desperate for answers, for something solid that might give him a lead, he checked under the bed, looked for cracks or gaps in the floor, walls and ceiling that might suggest a hiding spot where she'd stashed something. He checked the oven and microwave. The barbecue on the tiny patio.

Nada.

Stepping back inside he put his hands on his hips, mind racing. There was no way she could have cleared this place out alone last night after crashing into that lake. She'd have been near hypothermic, probably concussed if not worse, and on the run. He couldn't see a professional risking showing up here when it was only a five-minute drive from where he'd seen her crawl out of the water. Not with him so close.

She must have at least a passport or some other ID and other shit hidden somewhere, because she hadn't had anything with her except her clutch purse last night and there'd been nothing in it except a small amount of cash and a lipstick. No, his gut said she'd left something here and he just hadn't found it yet. If he was in her shoes she'd be heading out of the country as soon as possible.

For that she'd need documents, even if they were fake. If they were here, then she'd be coming back for them. She'd have known all about him long before last night, known what he was capable of and that he wouldn't give up the hunt.

Too much was at stake. So where the hell was she?

There'd been no sign of her at any hospital within a hundred miles of here. He had sources on the lookout for her at airports, bus stations, train stations, rental car companies, hotels. She apparently didn't have a handler or anyone to turn to in whatever agency had hired her.

She also couldn't have fucking disappeared into thin air. He figured she must have stolen a car, or had one already bought and waiting for her prior to last night.

After doing one more thorough look around and finding nothing, he left and headed for the SUV he'd parked in the underground garage. Anger pulsed through him as he drove back to his condo.

Unless one of his people got an alert on her—and he wasn't convinced that would happen considering her level of training—then her apartment was his only chance of finding her at the moment. He'd have to hope he was right, that she'd come back to get whatever she'd left behind. For now, he'd keep the building under constant surveillance.

All he needed was one strong lead. Once he found her, he'd take out his anger and humiliation on her body, pry out of her who in the CIA had hired her so he could feed that to the Big Boss and save his own skin.

Then he'd end her.

****

It sounded like he had a damn mini chainsaw going at the foot of his bed.

Wyatt expelled an exasperated sigh and rolled to his back, staring up at the darkened ceiling of his bedroom in the cabin. Grits might be little, but right now he sounded like an eighty-year-old man suffering from severe sleep apnea.

He glanced down at the dog, currently sprawled out on top of the patchwork quilt his grandmother had made. She'd hate to see it being covered in dog hair.

Grits let out another teeth-rattling snorfle, actually stopped breathing for a second or two before snorting and still didn't wake himself up.

Wyatt glared at him and nudged him with his foot. "Hey, mutton-head."

Grits twitched but kept on sawing logs. With a badly *rusted* chainsaw.

"Hey," he repeated, louder, his nudge less gentle this time. "Wake up."

The dog stopped snoring and lay there, tail wagging sleepily, thumping gently against the quilt.

"Dude, seriously, you're killing me. I'm the lightest sleeper you've ever met and this cannot go on." He'd been that way since his first combat deployment. Every tiny movement or sound woke him up and put him on alert. Pure survival instinct back then. Now it was habit. The struggle was real.

Wyatt reached for the dog, who lowered his head and wagged just the end of his tail, giving him a pitiful look in a clear plea to be allowed to stay on the bed.

Refusing to be sucked in just because of how cute the dog was, he picked him up and set him on the floor.

"You go sleep in your own bed." When Piper had dumped the little guy on his doorstep, Wyatt had thought housetraining him would be the toughest part, but it turned out the real issue was not getting sucked into the whole big brown-eyed routine Grits pulled.

Grits gazed at him for a long moment, as though waiting for him to change his mind, then stood up on his hind legs. He put his front paws on the edge of the bed, his tail wagging madly, head cocked, ears perked. *Pretty please, can I stay? I'll be a good boy.*

"No. Bed." Wyatt pointed to the cushy dog bed he'd bought the day after Piper had brought Grits over. All dogs deserved a comfy bed. Spending the money on a memory foam mattress for Grits didn't mean Wyatt planned on keeping him.

Grits's ears flopped in disappointment. He dropped his front paws to the ground and turned away, his tail drooping, looking like the most dejected animal ever born. His nails clicked on the old plank floor as he slowly headed for his bed and curled up there with a mournful and slightly accusatory expression, as if Wyatt had banished him to the ends of the earth rather than the end of the room.

"Drama queen," Wyatt muttered, rolling over and stuffing his pillow into a more comfortable position. Dog was lucky Wyatt had kept him this long.

Five minutes later, Grits was snoring lightly and Wyatt was thinking about hunting down some earplugs. Freaking *earplugs*, just so he could sleep in his own damn bed, in his own damn house. Because of a damn dog he hadn't asked for and didn't want.

And now he couldn't sleep. This time of night was always the hardest. Sometimes his dreams tormented him, but the ghosts never went away even when he was awake.

That hellish mission never let him go. It was always there in the back of his mind, just waiting to dig its claws into him. The guilt was way tougher to handle than the grief, and a thousand times harder to deal with than his injuries or the suffering he'd endured after.

Their faces were so clear to him. All the guys who had died that day on his watch. The agony and horror in their expressions as they'd died around him.

And Raider.

How that incredible, heroic dog had given her life to save Wyatt's.

Covered in a thin film of sweat, he sat up and dragged a hand over his face. Fuck. Was it ever going to get any easier? It was hell, reliving it over and over again. All the therapy in the world wouldn't erase his memories, and it sure as hell wouldn't soothe his conscience. Those men and Raider had died that day because he'd fucked up. Their deaths were all on him.

Shoving the sheet and quilt off, he swung his legs over the side of the bed and reached for his prosthesis where it rested against the nightstand. Grits jumped out of his bed and came racing over, tail waving and body wiggling with excitement.

Wyatt ignored him, another arrow of guilt slicing through him when he looked at that adorable little face. He'd sworn he'd never get another dog, that he wouldn't replace Raider out of respect for her memory and the sacrifice she'd made.

He really needed to call Piper and tell her he wasn't ready for a dog, make her come take Grits. It was better for Grits that way. Things were busy enough around here, and the last thing Wyatt needed was another responsibility.

Such as an unwanted female houseguest who might pose a security threat to his family.

Frowning, he thought about this woman, Trinity, his brother had brought home. Who the hell was she and just what kind of trouble was she in? He didn't like unknowns and didn't appreciate a stranger possibly bringing trouble to his dad and brother, let alone on their own property that had been in the family since before the Civil War.

After putting on the protective sock around the stump that ended just below his right knee, he pulled on the artificial leg, standing to ease what was left of his tibia down into the base of the socket. The titanium-carbon piece that served as his new foot bent and flexed with each step.

Naked, he strode to the armoire that functioned as his closet, dragged out jeans and a T-shirt then put them on. He was on his way to the kitchen to find something to eat when Grits suddenly stilled and perked his ears, looking toward the cabin's front door.

The back of Wyatt's neck prickled, his training kicking in. He watched the dog closely, noted the alert posture. Then Grits let out a soft *woof* and ran to the front door.

On guard, Wyatt went to the window beside the door and pulled the curtain aside. Sure as hell, a figure emerged out of the shadows alongside the house and started across the lawn.

Curvy. Unmistakably female.

Brody's houseguest had apparently tired of their brand of Southern hospitality. Where was she sneaking off to at this time of night?

I don't think so, sweetheart.

Shoving on his boots, he reached for the door handle.

Chapter EIGHT

Trinity waited until it was full dark before carefully easing her bedroom door open. The hours she'd spent waiting to ensure that Brody and his father would be fast asleep had felt like an eternity. It was nearly two in the morning now, and the house had been still and quiet for a long time.

Pausing by her door, she waited there in the darkness for a few minutes to make sure no one had heard her, then crept down the stairs, careful to avoid the third one from the bottom, which she'd learned squeaked. This short reprieve from her dangerous, solitary life had been unexpected and wonderful, but she'd been here a full day already and it was high past time she headed out on her own again.

From the minute she'd arrived here she'd known she had to leave within a few days, but this afternoon with Brody had clinched it. She needed to get the hell away from him before they got even more involved.

She still couldn't believe she'd fallen asleep in his

arms. In her entire life she'd never done that, had never let her guard down that much with a man. She could blame her serious lack of judgment on her injuries and exhaustion, or on her stunning reaction to his kisses, but that was a cop out and she had never been one to shy away from the cold, hard truth.

She trusted him. And she wanted him.

Trinity honestly didn't know which one scared her more. That was all the motivation she needed to get gone.

A tiny part of her felt badly for sneaking out like this after all Brody had done for her, but it was necessary. Clean break. Move on. Back to the real world.

It didn't matter that part of her wanted to stay in this idyllic place a little longer, or that she wished she could find out exactly where the attraction burning between them would go. Putting distance between them, figuring out a way to go back to her apartment undetected and getting out of the country before Tino or anyone working for him found her was her one and only priority.

Once this was over with, though... God, she was tired of running, of being used, of wanting a "normal" life.

She made it as far as the side yard when she heard a telltale jingle behind her. She froze and glanced over her shoulder. Grits was racing toward her, ears flopping up and down in the moonlight, mouth open, tongue lolling. Behind him she saw a large, familiar silhouette detach itself from the shadows surrounding the cabin.

Shit.

"Out for a little moonlight stroll?" Wyatt called out, his gruff voice cutting through the quiet like a blade.

Yes. To get far away from your brother. "I've got things to take care of."

He paused a few feet away and put his hands in his

pockets. "Brody know you're leaving?"

Pretty obvious that he didn't. "Just tell him thanks for me." She turned to walk away and the back door of the main house opened. *Dammit...*

"Where are you going?" Brody said behind her, his voice accusing.

Trinity pulled in a breath and fought for patience. How the hell had Wyatt even heard her? She was stealth personified when she wanted to be, and she'd definitely wanted to be.

Bracing herself, she turned around to face Brody. And damn it, her heart squeezed at the sight of him rushing toward her in a pair of jeans and tugging a shirt over his head. She shot an annoyed look at Wyatt. "What are you even doing up right now?"

He shrugged. "I don't sleep much. Grits heard you leave. Guess he's a better guard dog than I thought."

She transferred her gaze to the dog, who was wiggling happily in front of her, clearly hoping for a pat. "Thanks a lot," she muttered to him.

Brody strode across the lawn toward her, the moonlight showing the frown on his face. "Where the hell are you going?"

"Town." Where she had planned to steal a car to get her through the mountains. That would put enough time and distance between them so that she could think clearly again.

"And do what? You've got no money, no ID, no bank cards." He eyed her, shook his head once. "Just how many crimes were you planning on committing to get away from me?" His tone vibrated with frustration.

Her jaw clenched. "I'm not 'getting away from you'. I've got things to do and I have to do them alone."

Rather than answer, Brody shot his brother a pointed look. Wyatt muttered a gruff goodbye, then whistled for Grits to follow him as he walked away. The dog raced after him, ears and tail flopping.

As soon as they were alone and Wyatt was out of earshot, Brody stepped closer, took her arm. Trinity tensed and pulled out of reach. He stopped, set his hands on his hips and looked at her. "Is this because of what happened earlier?"

She'd never admit that. "I have to get back to D.C. tonight."

"To D.C., where everyone will be looking for you?"

She barely held her frustration in check. He was right, but she had to face the risk at some point and at the moment she felt the driving impulse to get away from Brody and what he made her feel. She already cared about him too much. "I need to get to my apartment." The place she'd stayed at as herself, before adopting Eva Gregorivich's persona.

"Why?" A demand, not a question.

"I need some things there to get out of the country." She would have to do it using a new alias and the disguise she'd hidden at the apartment.

His expression grew even more troubled. "Why not contact whoever hired you for help? You did the job, so surely they could grab whatever you need or arrange to get you out of the country safely."

"They won't." That was made crystal clear to her before she'd signed the contract. Which they'd no doubt disposed of by now. "Because I was seen, I've burned all my bridges with the people who hired me. There's no one to help me, I have to go back and do this myself."

Brody folded his arms across his chest, the move drawing her unwilling gaze to the mouthwatering size and shape of his body. "I don't like the thought of you going back there alone."

"I can take care of myself. Been doing it a long time."

"Yeah. But you don't need do it alone this time.

You've got me."

For a moment she was too stunned to speak. "You don't even know me," she said finally, unable to keep the rough edge out of her voice. The way he freely offered to step up and help her made her feel raw, vulnerable even.

He shrugged a thick shoulder. "I know enough."

"No, you really don't. So thank you for everything you've done, but I won't let you do more."

He raised an eyebrow, his gaze pinning her in place. "Who says you've got a choice in the matter? I'm already involved and I intend to see this through, at least make sure you get out of D.C. safely. I've got contacts I can reach out to, they can help us—"

"*No.*" It was unbelievable that he'd do this. To risk so much. His family was here and he was supposed to be recuperating from his injury.

He settled a warm palm on the side of her face, the gesture protective, tender. It turned her heart over. "Hasn't there ever been anyone who cared about you? Anyone who was willing to watch your back?"

Just my Valkyrie sisters. She was desperate enough to contact them but Briar was in L.A., and last she'd heard, Georgia was in Cuba. Both were too far away to help her.

Unable to find her voice because of the sudden lump in her throat, she shook her head.

Brody lowered his hand and she missed his touch immediately. "Well, like I said. You've got me this time. I'll drive you back once we come up with a plan. And I'm not up to planning something like that at the moment—it's two in the damn morning. Come on." He pivoted and began walking away.

She had to put a stop to this hero complex thing he had going. It was too crazy. "Brody."

"What?" He didn't bother turning around.

"I can't let you do this."

"Sorry, not changing my mind."

She hit him where she knew it would hurt. "Your family needs you. They've suffered enough without anything else happening to you."

He stopped, slowly turned back to face her. "Yeah, they have. But that also means they'll understand because they wouldn't want you to go back and face this thing alone."

She threw her hands up in exasperation. "God, you're so freaking stubborn!"

"Yep. Now come on."

She stared after him for a long moment, silently stewing. The element of surprise she'd been so certain she had was long gone. Even if she made a break for it now, she wouldn't make it to the end of the driveway before he caught her, bum leg or not. And dammit, he'd hit her where it hurt too, by telling her she didn't have to go it alone this time. Had he sensed her loneliness somehow? She would rather die than have him pity her.

Huffing out an annoyed breath, she grudgingly followed. "Where are we going?" she grumbled, frowning as she followed him across the lush back lawn toward the horse paddock behind the house.

"For a walk."

"A walk?" Was he serious?

"My leg's stiffened up."

For a fleeting moment she considered running for it, then felt bad, gave in and followed. She caught up to him in just a few strides and walked next to him, comforted by the weight of the pistol she'd tucked into the back of her waistband. She'd lived most of her life looking over her shoulder everywhere she went and it was no different here, even with Brody beside her. "How were you wounded?"

"During an op in Jordan this past January. The

entire team was in a tight spot and I caught a bullet during the firefight before we got evacuated."

She eyed his legs as he walked, noted the increased hitch in his stride. "How bad was it?"

"Still got my leg," he answered, as if that said everything. "I'm missing a chunk of muscle in my thigh, but I can still get by."

Not something minor, then. He'd have had at least one surgery to repair the damage. "So you'll be able to rejoin your team one day?"

"Not sure yet, but I sure as hell hope so." He stopped at the fence beyond the cabin where Wyatt lived, laid his forearms on the top rail. Two horses wandered toward them, ears pricked. "While we're sharing information, what's a Valkyrie?"

"The same thing as Briar."

"Which is?"

She cast him a measured glance. "Matt never told you?"

He shook his head, his eyes intent on her. His nearness was affecting her, impossible to ignore. Strong and capable. "I know she works for the NSA and can handle herself in the field with a long gun. That's pretty much all I know about her operational capability."

Trinity stared back at him, refusing to look away, trying to figure out what his ulterior motive was. Everyone had one. But again, telling him about this part of her past cost her nothing. Not given who he was and what he did for a living. Besides, he'd be gone from her life soon enough anyway, would never see her again. After everything he'd done and offered, it was only fair that he knew what she was and what she was running from because of the possible threat to him and his family.

The horses had reached the fence now. She began petting one of them, found it easier to avoid looking at

Brody as she answered. "The Valkyrie Project was a secret CIA program that recruited young girls with no means or family and trained them to become assassins."

She sensed his shock in the taut silence that spread between them but he didn't say anything, so she continued. "They recruited me when I was nine, took me out of foster care and put me into the program. We had trainers from various SOF branches, and from every intelligence agency in the country. After graduation I worked for them until I turned twenty-seven, then went out on my own."

"So you, Briar and Georgia are government-trained assassins," he repeated.

She nodded.

"You said you're not a designated sniper like the other two. Then what are you, exactly?"

"Pretty sure you've already read between the lines enough to figure that out on your own." She cringed inside, hating that she cared what he'd think of her for it.

For a moment he didn't answer. "They hired you to seduce Salvatori, so you could kill him up close and personal."

She dipped her head in acknowledgement. "I came to D.C. a couple months ago and arranged an introduction under an alias I created." The prep work for that stage alone had taken her months.

"Why do it?" he asked, sounding puzzled. "For the money?"

"Not entirely." Though the money was decent and went into an offshore account. She donated a good chunk of it to various charities. In particular, one that assisted sexual abuse and sex trafficking survivors. A cause close to her heart. "I turn down more jobs than I take. I like being able to choose my targets."

"So it's personal for you."

"In a way."

She tensed when he slid a hand into the back of her hair, but made herself hold her ground and look at him. To her surprise she found not horror or judgment in his expression, but concern. "You said Salvatori was into sex trafficking. Is that why you took the job?"

"Mostly, yes." It was her opportunity to settle the score. This way she could stop some of the monsters from hurting more victims. She was helping protect the innocent, because no one had protected her.

He stepped closer, his big body inches from hers, a frown pulling at his brow. "Did someone...hurt you like that? In the past?" His eyes held a buried anger now.

She glanced away and resumed petting the horse, hating this conversation but liking the feel of his hand on her and the balm of his concern all too much. If anyone in her life had cared one tenth as much about her back when she was a kid, things might have turned out so much differently. She might have been...normal. Maybe even happy.

"Did they?" he pressed, his voice soft but with a lethal edge she recognized.

She pulled free of his hand. "They did what they felt was necessary to turn me into what I am today."

His eyes widened in outrage. "Wait, you're saying your *trainers* did it?"

She glanced away. While the CIA had technically founded the program, they'd given their trainers a certain...operational latitude with the trainees, and turned a blind eye while they implemented their unorthodox methods. Then someone had gone too far.

"One of them." And she'd never forget his face. "He was a contract agent. All our trainers were. They weren't held to the same...ethical standards as the actual agents were."

On her fifteenth birthday one of her trainers had shown her what would happen if she couldn't defend herself against a man. He'd taught her what it meant to be physically at the mercy of a man while he used her body and she was helpless to stop it. It had been her first sexual experience and it had left one hell of a lasting impression.

The brutal lesson had been permanently ingrained into her psyche: always be in control, never let anyone use you again. It had hardened her, inside and out. Since then, she never underestimated her targets. Never let her guard down, never let them have the upper hand. She never let a man in.

She held the power. *She* was the one in control. Always.

"I don't believe this." He sounded horrified. "Why the hell would you ever work for the government again after what they did to you?"

"Because this way I can even the odds." She was a Valkyrie—and just like the mythical Norse females they were named after, *she* got to choose who lived and died on the battlefield. "He paid for what he did. He was fired from the program and served jail time." And then he'd met with an unfortunate…accident a few years after his release.

Brody didn't say anything to that, simply cursed under his breath and paced a few steps away.

His reaction shouldn't have hurt, yet it did. He was no doubt disgusted, and she understood his shock. She wasn't ashamed of her past, of what she was, but she rarely told anyone the truth because she didn't want to risk the judgment and rejection.

She put on a wry smile to cover the burn in her chest. "Not so tempting any more, am I?"

Brody swiveled his head to meet her gaze and the look on his face wiped the smile away. In the moonlight his eyes burned with a cold fury and his jaw was knotted. But he wasn't angry at her, she realized with a start. He was angry at what had happened to her so long ago.

"Fuck them," he ground out after a charged moment. "Fuck them all for doing that to you. For being part of it, and for letting it happen in the first place."

She folded her arms and stared at the horses, trying to ward off the sudden chill that rippled over her skin. No one had ever cared about what happened to her, except maybe Briar and Georgia, the only two people on earth who knew her darkest secrets, who understood her and accepted the stains on her soul. "It made me stronger."

"It shouldn't have happened *period*. Jesus." He walked another few paces away, ran a hand through his hair.

It shouldn't have mattered to her that he cared so much, but it did, touching the deeply buried wound she'd locked away inside her where no one else could see.

No. Stop. There's no way this can go anywhere. You'll be gone in a matter of days and he'll forget all about you.

She suppressed her burgeoning feelings out of habit, refused to let them cloud her judgment as she narrowed her eyes in warning. "Don't you dare pity me."

He swung around to face her, his eyebrows drawn together in a fierce frown. "I don't pity you. I'm pissed as hell that our government would do that to an innocent girl. And you should be too."

An unexpected lump lodged in her throat and she had to look away again. She lived with the memory and outrage every day of her life. But with Brody looking that way at her right now, all of a sudden she felt…dirty, in a way she hadn't since the rape. After only one full day with him, he'd already managed to crack the walls she'd been forced to erect around herself, out of necessity.

Out of survival.

When she turned away, intending to walk back to the house, he caught her arm. She gritted her teeth and pulled free but he just caught her again and tugged her around.

He set both hands on her shoulders, ran them gently up and down her arms, raising goose bumps. "That should never have happened to you. And, God...I wish I could go back in time and shoot the bastards responsible."

At his words, something shifted inside her. A kind of thawing, deep in the center of her chest. "He's dead now."

His hands paused on her upper arms. "Did you kill him?"

It made her grin, him sounding so hopeful about that. "What do you think?"

"I hope you did, because the son of a bitch deserved it," he answered flatly.

Oh, she had. She'd hunted him down as soon as she'd left the Valkyrie program, shortly after he'd been released from prison. At a bar in downtown Portland, Maine, she'd slipped poison into his beer while he'd been trying to pick up another woman to abuse.

When he'd dropped to the floor and grabbed for his throat, she'd stepped into his line of sight, made sure he saw her before he died. Watching the knowledge of what she'd done dawn in his eyes in the moments before he took his last breath made it by far the most satisfying kill of her life.

"Hey," he murmured, bringing her out of the memory.

She let out a deep breath as those incredible hands moved up to her neck now, stroked the sides of it before they cradled her head.

His dark eyes delved into hers and she was too spellbound to pull away. "Tell me it wasn't always like that for you. Tell me there's been someone along the way who showed you not all men are like that."

Why did he care so much? She lowered her gaze to his chest, unable to look him in the eye as she answered. "Once," she whispered after a tense pause. "A long time ago." Back when she'd been young and still somehow naïve, despite her brutal training experience. For a while she'd even thought she might be falling in love with him.

Until reality had hit her in the face and shown her the truth of who he really was. "But he wound up selling me out because he was afraid for his own safety." She looked up at him.

His gaze hardened like steel. "Then the gutless asshole didn't deserve you."

But you do? She bit back the words at the last possible moment, too afraid of his answer, because she was pretty sure he'd say yes. And she was having a hard enough time resisting him as it was.

"Lucky for me, I don't scare easy," he murmured, his eyes on hers.

A ribbon of longing twisted painfully around her heart at the same time as heat curled in her abdomen. She didn't resist his hold, even allowed her eyes to close when he leaned down to settle his mouth over hers.

This time the kiss was gentle, tender. An offer of comfort. A promise to protect and cherish.

The ribbon twisted harder, until her entire chest ached.

Before she could reach for him or deepen the kiss to turn it into something more, he pulled away and captured her hand, twining his fingers through hers. For some reason it felt like more of a claiming than his kisses had.

"We'll come up with something together in the

morning," he said. "It's late. Let's sleep on it first." With a gentle tug he led her back toward the house, and she was powerless to resist.

Chapter NINE

A s a precaution to make sure Trinity didn't try another escape attempt under cover of darkness, Brody had camped out on the couch all night. Sixteen hours later, his leg still hurt like a bitch.

He was on the floor doing his stretches when her light footfalls came down the stairs. She paused at the bottom, looking fresh after her shower. "Sore?" she asked.

"A little." He sat up, grimacing a bit as his stiff muscles pulled. "It's just us here again." His dad was in town getting some supplies and Wyatt was at a VA appointment in the D.C. area. Brody had told them he'd be taking Trinity back to D.C. at some point today. "You ready to go?"

"Yeah, but keep stretching. I'll put on some coffee." She headed into the kitchen.

Brody resumed his stretches and watched her as she worked. She was moving more fluidly today and the swelling in her face had gone way down. He couldn't help but admire her shapely curves while she stood with her back to him at the counter.

When she lifted on tiptoe to reach into one of the cupboards and turned slightly, the hem of her borrowed sweater rode up, exposing the creamy expanse of her stomach. He'd lain awake for a good hour last night after coming back into the house, thinking of what she'd told him about her past.

It enraged him to think that a government agency would stand by and allow the sort of abuse Trinity had suffered. He ached to think of her enduring that, would give anything for the chance to replace that horrific memory with a good one.

The rich scent of brewing coffee drew him out of his thoughts. He pushed to his feet and headed over to her.

She glanced at him, those deep blue eyes pulling him in. "You take a bit of cream, right?"

"Yeah." He wasn't surprised she remembered that from yesterday. Operators watched their surroundings carefully and noticed details.

She added some cream to his coffee and offered him the mug. He made sure his fingers lingered on hers at the transfer, was rewarded by a delicate pink blush that stole into her cheeks.

"Thanks," he murmured, glad that she was as affected by their chemistry as he was. She'd already booked a flight to London in the morning using an alias and a credit card belonging to that persona she'd memorized the number of.

If he had his way, she'd be spending her last night in the States naked in his bed at his place near Quantico. He wasn't ready to let her go yet. There was something special brewing between them and he wanted to see where it led.

He joined her at the table, leaned back in his chair.

"So, anything else you want to go over?" They'd already planned things out this morning. Well, *she'd* planned things. He'd been careful to let her run the show so she wouldn't pull back from him, and he hadn't had any objections to anything she'd said, so he'd kept quiet.

"We didn't talk about what would happen once I retrieve my gear."

"No, we didn't." Because he was still hoping all would go smoothly and he'd be able to convince her to stay the night with him. He wanted much more than one night, but if that's all he could have, he'd take it.

She lowered her gaze to her mug. "After I get my things we go our separate ways—"

"I'm not leaving you until you get on your flight out of the country," he informed her, not about to keep silent on that point. "That part's not up for negotiation."

For a moment it looked like she would argue but then she sighed and relented. "All right, but if this thing goes sideways, you have to promise me that we'll split up and you'll get clear."

"Why London?" he asked instead, avoiding that promise because he didn't want to lie to her. There was no way he was leaving her to fend for herself if things got ugly.

"I'm based there, for now. I've lived there for the past year or so."

Made it damn hard for him to see her again, and he definitely wanted to. He might not know her all that well, but he knew enough. He'd make sure she was safe tonight and personally see her onto the plane tomorrow night.

She finished her coffee and set her mug down, eyeing him across the table. "You sure about this?"

"Yeah," he said, an edge to his voice. He was tired of her trying to come up with a reason to ditch him. "Thought I made that pretty damn clear already."

"All right." She stood, grabbed both mugs and carried them to the sink. "Let's roll then."

He had his gear already stowed in a lockbox in the back of his truck. Fatigues, helmet, body armor, rifle, pistols, ammo and medical supplies. Trinity had insisted on seeing it all that afternoon. They were both carrying a concealed pistol with them as they climbed into the truck.

He drove them through town as darkness fell over the valley, then headed east toward the mountains.

"Will you be coming back here for a while after?" she asked him.

"Most likely." He still hadn't been able to have the downtime he'd been so looking forward to, and there were plenty of things he could help out his dad and Wyatt with on the property.

"Do Charlie and Easton come home much?"

"Charlie more so. She works in D.C. Easton's job comes with a demanding schedule and he travels a lot. He and I both like to come home for downtime when we can, and I know my dad likes to have us around. Even if he says we're pains in his ass sometimes."

"You're lucky," she murmured, staring out her window. "To have a home and family like that."

"I know." He felt bad that she had neither and decided to change the subject. "After we go to the apartment. Where are you planning on staying?"

"I'll find a hotel."

Fortune favored the brave, or so the saying went. "My place is just outside Quantico. Stay there with me tonight." He glanced over in time to see her swivel her head to look at him, the streetlamps they passed revealing the guarded expression on her face.

"I don't think that's such a good idea."

"Why not," he said, trying to sound casual. Her rejection stung, even if he'd been expecting it.

"I'm leaving tomorrow night and we won't ever see each other again."

If that's the way she wanted to leave things, then he'd have to accept it. But he at least wanted tonight with her. He'd never experienced chemistry like this before, and she'd already gotten under his skin. "Just think about it," he said.

She didn't answer, instead turning her attention back out her window.

Being a Sunday night, there was little traffic on the road. The two-hour drive passed far too quickly, and then they were on the outskirts of D.C. He drove her to a costume shop they'd checked online earlier and went in with her while she gathered pieces for her disguise.

"I'll pay you back," she said as she carried everything to the checkout. "I've got cash at my place."

He didn't want her damn money, but withheld the words and handed the clerk his credit card. Once they were in the truck he stayed up front while she climbed into the backseat to change. When she slid into the front passenger seat a few minutes later he did a double take. She looked like a completely different person.

She had on light blue nursing scrubs that concealed the shapely curves he loved so much. A light brown wig hid her sharp black bob, and she'd tied the long waves into a low ponytail that fell past her shoulder blades.

There were no visible bruises on her face anymore. She'd used some kind of makeup to make her eyebrows match her hair, to make her eyes appear more deeply set, and she'd somehow altered the appearance of her nose too. Her cheekbones seemed sharper as well, and whatever she'd done with the pale lipstick made her full lips look thinner. The running shoes she'd borrowed from Briar completed the outfit.

The startling transformation in so short a time was impressive, but he had the strangest urge to pull that wig off, wipe the makeup away so he could see *her*.

"Do I look okay?"

He met her gaze and was confronted once again by the stark truth. She'd done this a thousand times before—disguised herself and seduced whatever information she needed out of a target before either disappearing or killing him.

He understood it, even respected it to a certain degree, but he didn't like that she'd been forced to do it and he didn't buy the tough act completely, because he'd seen the real Trinity over the past two days. He'd even managed to put a few cracks in the walls she'd erected around herself, giving him glimpses of the woman behind the mask.

Part of him wanted to destroy those walls completely, while another part warned that she was still a highly skilled chameleon. A lethal one. Even if he saw her again and they moved into some sort of a relationship, a part of him would always wonder if she was being truthful with him. He had to remember that.

"Yeah, you look good. I wouldn't have recognized you if you'd walked past me on the sidewalk," he said and started the engine.

"Well, if he's out there, hopefully Tino won't either."

Yeah. Hopefully. He steered out of the parking lot. "All right. Where to?"

Brody followed her directions to an area on the outskirts of the city, to an older brick apartment building in a rougher neighborhood.

"Turn left at the next corner and drive past it," she said, clearly in operational mode as he approached the stoplight. When it turned green he had to pause to let two pedestrians cross the intersection before driving past the building with Trinity surveying the sidewalks carefully.

He counted three hookers standing on one corner, and guys who looked like drug dealer-types on another. "Why did you pick an apartment here?" he asked, disliking the thought of her staying in such a sketchy area alone, training or not.

"People in this kind of neighborhood tend to ignore each other and just go about their business, and not ask questions."

"See anything?" he asked, watching all his mirrors. He'd been on high alert since reaching the city, but he hadn't noticed any sign that someone might be following them and even if someone happened to see them entering her apartment building, there was no way they'd recognize her.

"No. Turn right at the next light and double back, but take a different route this time."

"Not my first recon job," he said, cutting her a sharp look before doing as she said. Nothing caught his attention as he did the second pass.

He made two more after that, taking different routes, and still didn't notice anything suspicious. Someone might have noticed him repeatedly driving past the building, but the chances were low. "Okay?" he asked her.

She nodded once. "Okay. Pull around back. I'm going to go in the side entrance. Fewer security cameras there."

Brody parked in a spot behind the building, making sure to leave plenty of space in front of them in case they had to make a quick getaway. He killed the engine and glanced around the area, seeing nothing but parked cars and a Dumpster set against the building.

"You'll carry the bag?" she asked.

"Yeah." He reached into the back and withdrew a backpack that held more pistols, ammo and the tools she'd need to get into the building and apartment. He gazed up at the building's rough exterior. "How old is this place?" He didn't like the thought of her living here, alone. This was the rough kind of place where everyone who lived here looked the other way when something bad happened. It might be what she wanted but he didn't have to like it.

"Ancient." She glanced at him and he had another jolt of surprise at just how different she looked. "Ready?"

"Ready." He got out first, circled around the front of the truck and kept his eyes on the street next to the building. Trinity stepped out. He couldn't see a bulge beneath her scrubs but he knew she was armed with at least one pistol.

At the side entrance he kept watch while she stood in the shadows and used a tool to jimmy the locks free. The old metal door creaked as it swung open with a rush of musty air hitting him.

She paused to look around then waved him forward. He followed her up the stairs, every sense on alert, one hand at the small of his back to draw his weapon at the first hint of danger.

Together they checked to make sure each flight of stairs was clear before climbing them. On the sixth floor she cracked the stairwell door open and scanned the dimly lit hallway. Up here the air reeked of cigarette smoke and stale food. The carpet looked shabby and the paint on the walls was chipped.

Brody followed close behind her as she headed to the right and began walking down the hallway. He deciphered every sound coming from the apartments they passed, dismissing them as threats one by one. The murmur of voices inside the apartments they passed. A TV in the background. A baby's cry.

At the second apartment from the end Trinity stopped and checked the door and frame. Apparently satisfied that all was as it should be, she made short work of the lock and pushed the door open a few inches. Brody waited, noting the tension in her body. Then it faded and she pressed the door open.

"Come on," she said. "Looks like the coast is clear."

But he heard the note of suspicion in her voice. She was still on edge. He stayed behind her and shut the door after them, then helped her sweep the place.

Empty.

Relaxing slightly, he tailed her into the bedroom, aware of the unease coiling in the pit of his stomach. They'd gotten in without a problem. He just hoped getting out would be as smooth.

****

Tino jackknifed into a sitting position on his couch when the new ringtone went off on his phone. Those notes could only mean one thing.

He grabbed it from the coffee table, heart thumping, and checked the app he'd installed to verify. Yep. Someone had just triggered the motion detector at the apartment Trinity Durant had stayed in prior to becoming Eva Gregorivich.

He shot to his feet and rushed to the hall closet for his go bag, already making the call as he stepped out into the hallway and raced for the stairs. "Someone's there," he told the man. "Where are you?"

"Outside across the street. I saw a couple people go through the side door a few minutes ago but it didn't look like her so I stayed here."

"A couple?"

"Yeah. Man and woman. She was wearing nursing scrubs."

He was already out at the curb, heading for his

SUV. "Did they show up in a vehicle?"

"Yeah, I marked the plate number down. I'll text it to you."

"Good. Now get in there and check it out. I'm on my way, should be there in six or seven minutes." Anticipation roared through his veins in a heady rush. He now knew just how good Trinity was with disguises. Had to be her. Who was the man with her?

"You think it's her?" his Mob contact asked, sounding dubious. Tino had brought him into this because the man needed the extra money and had done jobs like this one before.

"Someone just triggered the motion detector, and yeah, I think it's her." There was no reason for anyone else to be entering that shit-bag apartment, and he knew the landlord hadn't rented it out to anyone else yet. "Don't let them leave. Take him out if you need to, but remember I want her alive. Text me what you've got so far."

He ended the call and tossed his go bag into the front passenger seat, thought about the set of instruments he'd packed in preparation. Scalpels and pliers, other neat tools that he could play with while he interrogated her.

He'd get the name of whoever had hired her, and find out why they'd gone after Salvatori. Once he fed that to the Big Boss, the pressure on him would ease.

Tino's heart beat faster as he sped down the street, already imagining what it would feel like to have her helpless and at his mercy. In another few minutes he'd get the bitch and make her pay for what she'd done to him.

First he'd fuck her, then he'd administer the suffering she had coming.

And when he'd grown bored of her cries and pleas, he'd end her. Then he'd dump her body in a public place as a warning to the CIA or any other government agency that the Mob wasn't to be fucked with.

Chapter TEN

While Brody stood guard from the bathroom doorway, Trinity lay down on the cracked linoleum floor and rolled to her back to access the secret compartment she'd made inside the cabinet beneath the sink. With her Leatherman tool she pried away the piece of wood holding the board in place and set it beside her.

Reaching up into the gap, she felt around until she located the envelope she'd stashed here a few months ago. Then she retrieved the rifle components and magazine she'd hidden with it.

Sitting up, she checked to make sure everything was still in the envelope, including the passport and other ID for the identity she'd booked her upcoming flight under.

"All good?"

She looked up at Brody, felt that increasingly familiar jolt of desire and longing when she met his eyes. He'd asked her to spend the night with him. At his place. Part of her desperately wanted to seize the opportunity. The other part knew it was a bad idea. She was already way too attached to him as it was, and sleeping with him would only make it worse.

Then again, she was leaving in the morning, would likely never see him again, so what harm would a few hours in his bed do?

Yeah, even she didn't believe that lie. She knew damn well she'd wind up even more attached, but her gut said it would be worth it. "Yes."

Scooting onto her back to replace the board and strip of wood inside the cabinet, she could feel his gaze on her. An almost electric tingle spread over her skin, tightening her breasts and igniting a throb between her legs.

She hadn't enjoyed sex in a damn long time, but she instinctively knew she would with him. He'd already proven how unselfish he was, how willing he was to give her pleasure, ease her pain. If the man was half as good in bed as his kisses suggested, then yeah, she'd do a hell of a lot more than just enjoy it.

She slid out of the cabinet and climbed to her feet, shutting the door with her foot as she faced Brody. Damn he was sexy standing there guarding her, his body and skills honed by years of training and discipline. Ever since graduating from the Valkyrie program she'd worked alone and preferred it that way, but she had to admit it was nice to know that she had Brody here to watch her six on this one.

And she couldn't help but wonder if those formidable skills translated into the bedroom, and was pretty sure they did.

She knew all about sex. What moves to make to get a man into bed. How to drive him insane with pleasure and make him beg until he was completely powerless to her and her skill, craving the release she could give if she chose. While she remained completely unaffected.

What she didn't know was what it felt like to be on the receiving end of that sort of scenario. Or what it would be like to have a lover who knew her and cared about her. Someone who wanted to give pleasure as well as receive it, and share an intimacy she'd never allowed herself to experience before.

Watching Brody now, it was a tantalizing idea. He'd touched her gently, kissed her with both passion and tenderness that melted her brain and curled her toes. The thought of his mouth and those big, talented hands sliding over her naked body sent a shiver of arousal through her.

She shoved the distracting thought aside. They weren't out of danger yet and she still hadn't decided whether she wanted to stay the night with him or not. "All set."

His dark eyes assessed her for a long moment, asking that very question, and she knew he was every bit as aware of time slipping away. Her time with him was almost at an end and she had to make the decision soon.

"Okay." She handed him the envelope, then the rifle components. He put everything into the bag and slid one strap over a broad shoulder.

His phone buzzed. He glanced at the screen then answered, doing an assessing sweep of the apartment from the doorway. "Hey. You still in D.C.?"

Wyatt.

A pause. "I'm with Trinity. She's flying out tomorrow night."

Definitely Wyatt.

Trinity edged past him, his deliciously clean scent not helping her keep her libido under control. She headed for the front door, but stopped dead when something metallic scraped against the lock.

Without looking back, she motioned at Brody, who

immediately fell silent, phone still to his ear. In one second he was at her side, his attention riveted to the door, phone at his side.

The scraping came again and the doorknob slowly began to turn.

Brody drew his weapon but she grabbed his arm and ran for the window. She shoved it open and jumped onto the metal fire escape just as the apartment door opened.

Brody hopped down next to her and released the steel ladder with a clang. Looking back into the apartment, she caught a glimpse of a man with a weapon in his hand an instant before she whirled away.

"Go," Brody ordered her, one big hand pushing between her shoulder blades.

There wasn't time to argue about who went first. She mounted the rails, hooking her legs around the sides, and slid down them rather than wasting precious seconds taking the steps. She ran for the corner of the building as Brody followed suit behind her, giving a muffled grunt of pain as he hit the ground.

His leg.

Even as the worried thought formed she half-turned, and saw in horror that he'd stumbled. Above him, the silhouette of the man approached the window. Brody fell to his hands and knees just as the man appeared in the window above.

Trinity drew her weapon, her heart lodging in her throat as the man took aim at Brody.

In every op she'd ever been on, she'd worked solo and only had to worry about herself. Now fear for Brody took over completely and she reacted without thinking.

She raised her pistol but the angle was wrong. She fired anyway, to alert the gunman to her presence and keep him away from Brody. "Look out!" she cried, hoping to at least warn Brody or draw the gunman's attention away from him.

The man whirled toward her and fired just as she ducked around the corner of the building. A split second later the round punched into the brick, mere inches from where her head had just been.

Brody.

She shot an anxious glance toward him, saw the back of him as he darted around the opposite corner of the building, away from the shooter. The sheer relief flooding her made her dizzy.

He angled his head around the corner so he could see her, his weapon up and ready. With one hand he signaled for her to stay there, then disappeared from view.

Where the hell was he go—

A clattering noise announced that the shooter was descending the fire escape.

Crouched on one knee around the corner, Trinity waited a few seconds then swung around and took aim. The man had his weapon pointed at her.

They fired at the same time. Trinity hit him in the arm as his bullet slammed into the brick in front of her. Shards of brick and mortar stung her cheek as she jerked back.

The roar of an engine to the right shattered the tense silence. A swath of light cut across the building on the other side of the alley.

She glanced up in time to see Brody's truck hurtling toward her, high beams on. She squinted and raised a hand to shield her eyes from the glare. The gunman did the same and staggered back a step before he whirled to take aim at the truck.

Trinity swung around to fire again but the man leaped out of the way as Brody barreled past him, missing him by inches. The tires squealed as he took the corner sharply and plunged to a rocking stop a few feet from her.

He leaned across the front seat to push the passenger door open. "Get in!"

She raced over and jumped in, staying low as Brody peeled away and shot down the alley. In the side mirror she glimpsed the gunman shoving to his feet and taking aim.

A sharp *pop* rang out as he fired behind them, but Brody was already turning again, swerving out onto the main street. The few people standing on the corner shouted and scattered out of the way but she didn't see the shooter and there was no vehicle coming after them.

"Are you okay?" Brody demanded as he sped away from the building.

"Yeah, I'm good. You?" Willing her heart rate to slow down, she scanned him, noted the way his jaw was clamped tight.

He glanced at the rearview mirror, everything about him alert. "Fine."

He wasn't, she could tell from his pinched expression. "You hurt your leg?"

"I said I'm fine." His voice was strained.

She let it go, kept checking the mirrors with him.

"Any idea who that was?" He got on the highway, heading away from the city.

"No, but I can almost bet he was one of Tino's." Traffic was steady but she didn't pick out the signs of an erratic driver trying to keep up with them. No one was veering in and out of traffic or trying dangerous passing. "I wounded him in the arm, but not sure how bad." Maybe bad enough that he wouldn't follow them.

She'd never risked her life on a maybe, however, and she wasn't going to start now.

"I don't see anyone following us," she said a moment later. Hard to be certain of that though, given all the cars behind them. "I've got no idea how anyone found us at the apartment. Maybe Tino is paying a neighbor to spy on the place or something." She also didn't know how many others were out there hunting for her.

"Think anyone called the cops back there?"

Given the seedy neighborhood, there was a possibility that no one had. "Not sure." She hesitated before adding, "Pick an exit and drop me off somewhere."

He made a sound of disbelief and shook his head, the muscles in his jaw jumping. "Not happening. Deal with it."

"He's probably got your plate number. You're not safe." Worry for him made her pulse thud hard in her throat.

He shot her a hard look. "Neither are you."

She bit back an impatient retort, checked the mirrors again. God, he'd almost been shot because of her. She didn't want anything to happen to him but he refused to listen to reason.

He aimed a sideways look at her. "We could go to the cops."

"No. No way." The cops might be on the lookout for them right now but there was no way she was going to them for help. She was supposed to be invisible right now. Nobody at the CIA was going to vouch for her or clear her name. And she didn't plan on going to jail for a hit she'd committed at the request of the U.S. government.

He gave a hard sigh then pulled out his phone and dialed someone with the press of a button. "Hey, we've got a situation," he said as he took the next exit and drove down a quiet road that was bordered by rural land on one side and well-spaced houses on the other. He detailed what had just happened. "I need you to switch vehicles with me, then hide my truck somewhere until I tell you it's safe to move it." He named a meeting place. "Meet me in ten min—"

Trinity's gaze cut to the side mirror as a white sedan suddenly appeared behind them, gaining speed. Her nape prickled in subconscious warning.

"Shit, we've got company. I'll call you back once I'm clear." Brody set the phone in his lap and hit the gas, running through a red light.

The white car ran it too, barely avoiding being T-boned by a minivan in the intersection. Brody sped to the next road and turned left, taking them away from the residential area and out into farmland.

Headlights flashed in the side mirror. The white sedan fishtailed as it turned onto the same road and raced after them.

Not wasting any time, Trinity undid her seatbelt and scrambled into the backseat.

"What are you doing?" Brody said, his voice sharp as he sped down the darkened road.

"I'm gonna get rid of our tail," she said, rummaging through the backpack on the floor.

"No, put your seatbelt back on. I'm gonna see if I can lose him."

She ignored him. Two seconds later she came up with the rifle parts she'd stashed at her apartment and began assembling them.

"Trinity," he snapped. "Put your damn seatbelt on."

Nope. The people after her weren't going to give up. Even if they outran this guy, he would keep coming after her. And there would be others, including Tino. She had to end this *now* and she wasn't going to waste time arguing.

A glance through the rear window showed the sedan still coming after them. But not for long.

Slamming the magazine into the lower receiver, she knelt on the right rear passenger seat and reached for the button that would lower the window.

"Shit!"

She didn't even have time to brace before Brody hit the brakes, sending her flying into the back of the front seat. Scrambling into a stable position, she gripped the back of the headrest in front of her with her free hand and peered through the gap between the front seats to see what the problem was.

An SUV had turned out of a side street ahead of them and was swerving into their lane.

It straightened and raced toward them, coming at them head on.

****

He had them trapped now.

Pure elation exploded in Tino's veins as he roared straight at the silver pickup holding Trinity and the guy she'd been with at the apartment.

Surprise, motherfuckers. He sneered as the truck plunged to a stop in the middle of the quiet road.

They wouldn't have expected this, for him to appear as if out of nowhere and cut them off. But he had, thanks to a running commentary on their position and movements from Dante. For that, Tino could almost forgive him for not killing the unknown man and capturing Trinity back at the apartment.

The silver truck tried to turn around on the narrow road, but the maneuver cost precious time the occupants didn't have. There was nowhere for them to go now, nowhere left to run. Dante was still behind them, blocking their rear. There were no side streets. No streetlights here, no sidewalks and no houses or potential witnesses to what would happen next. Only agricultural land stretching out toward the highway.

You're all mine now.

His dick was rock hard as he mentally counted down the remaining seconds and he aimed straight for the pickup, anticipation exploding through him like a drug.

In just a matter of moments he'd kill the driver. Then he'd drag that conniving bitch out of the truck, shoot her first if necessary to disarm her. He'd take her to the place he'd prepared last night, a place where no one would ever find them, and enjoy making all his fantasies about her a reality.

Chapter TWELVE

Brody hit the brakes when he saw the car had angled itself across the road, blocking their escape. They had only seconds to make their move.

"I'll take the car, you take the SUV," Trinity said, and threw open her door.

"Wait—" Brody began, but she was already out and heading to the rear of the truck, rifle to her shoulder. The SUV was still barreling toward them.

Fuck this.

He threw the transmission into park and jumped out after her. He didn't have time to get his rifle from the lock box in the bed of the pickup. Armed only with his pistol he crouched behind the engine block, using it as cover as he sighted over the hood while Trinity went after the car's driver.

Aiming for the SUV's driver's side windshield, he fired three shots. The vehicle veered to the right and screeched to a stop thirty yards away, and when the thin moonlight flashed across the windshield he saw the spider web pattern where his shots had impacted but not penetrated the glass.

Dammit.

Behind him, three sharp pops rang out, then Trinity fired a double tap. "You get him?" he called back, hating this.

With his guys, he wouldn't have been this worried. They all had military backgrounds, trained together damn near every day, could practically read each other's minds and anticipate each other's movements. It felt wrong on every level to leave Trinity to handle the other driver.

"Can't tell yet, he's hiding behind the trunk. You?"

"Windshield has bullet-resistant glass." He didn't like that she was exposing herself like this but had to trust she knew what she was doing because he couldn't fend off attacks from both sides alone.

Brody cast a desperate glance around. Here they were pinned down. The only other cover he could see was a barn off to the right, maybe fifty yards away on the other side of a cornfield. Outside the beams of the headlights it was dark enough that they might be able to make a break for it.

Ahead of him, the SUV's rear passenger door flew open. Brody took aim, ready to fire. Behind him Trinity fired another double tap. "Mine's down," she announced, voice steady. "Dead."

Her rushed footsteps came toward him, and the person in the SUV fired at him. Brody instinctively ducked as the bullets thunked into the hood of his truck, but thankfully the engine stopped them.

He crouched near the front fender and leaned out to return fire. A pained grunt answered the shot, then the man took off. Brody caught a glimpse of him as he darted away from the SUV, lost him in the darkness as the man ran for the ditch.

"He ran east," he told Trinity when she came up behind him. "Can you see him?" He couldn't.

"No. I just checked the car and there's no one else in it."

They had to make sure the SUV was empty before going after him. His instinct was to order her to stay put but that would not only piss her off, and she wouldn't listen anyway. "Let's clear the SUV and go after this son of a bitch."

"I've got you covered."

His left leg screamed in protest as he pushed to his feet. The impact from when he'd landed after sliding down that fire escape had set his recovery back. He limped forward, weapon up as he approached the SUV at an angle, Trinity right behind him, the muzzle of her rifle pointed over his shoulder.

A quick check ensured the SUV was empty. "Must have run for the barn," Brody said.

"No, there," she said, turning to aim her rifle at something in the field next to the road. Brody swung around, just as shots rang out.

"Down!" Reaching back, he shoved Trinity to the ground. She landed with a gasp, then he rolled on top of her, shielding her as the bullets hit the SUV behind them.

"Let me up," she ordered, shoving at him.

He slid off her, biting back a growl of pain as he got to his hands and knees. The ache in his thigh was so bad he could barely get the muscles to obey him. By the time he'd made it to his feet Trinity was already moving, racing for the ditch in front of them. She jumped into it just as more shots rang out from the field.

"Fucker," Brody snarled under his breath, wishing he had NVGs to see the bastard. He rushed after her as fast as his bum leg would allow, heart in his throat at knowing Trinity was going after the shooter without him there to back her up.

She was lying on her belly on the upward slope of the far side of the ditch when he reached the edge of it. Before he could say anything, she began leopard-crawling over the lip and lay there perfectly still as he began the descent down the steep side of the grassy ditch, cursing his limited mobility and speed.

Two more shots punched through the silence. She sucked in a breath and his heart seized.

Trinity!

He bit the shout back for fear of drawing the shooter's attention. His weakened leg gave out and he slipped, sliding back down as she suddenly burst to her feet and ran into the rows of cornstalks.

A burst of adrenaline blasted through him. He scrambled up the slope, determined to protect her and hunt that bastard down.

Trinity ran through the field, dodging cornstalks and uneven clumps of earth as she moved toward the shooter's last location. He'd made a fatal error by firing multiple shots at her. One of the bullets had impacted a rock or log or something and sent up bits of debris that had cut her arm.

He had a pistol. She had a rifle. And now that she was on him it was only a matter of time before she got him.

When she was on the hunt, she always caught her prey.

Brody's hushed footfalls approached behind her. She didn't look back or try to communicate with him. This was the critical point. The shooter was close, she could feel him out there, watching for her. While she didn't need backup, she liked knowing Brody was nearby and had her six out here in the darkness.

Brody was just behind her when she caught a flash of movement in the weak moonlight filtering through the cornstalks. Her feet were silent on the soft earth as she followed it, the butt of the rifle solid against her shoulder, cheek pressed to the side of the stock.

Through her night vision scope, she finally spotted him, crouched to her left, about twenty yards away. He was raising his pistol, ready for another shot but he never got the chance.

She aimed at the center of his chest and squeezed the trigger, firing two shots in rapid succession. He grunted and crumpled. "Got him," she said to Brody as he reached her, then moved forward, keeping her rifle trained on her target.

Cornstalks swished against her scrubs as she strode toward her prey. In seconds she was standing over top of him. The man lay twisted on his side in the dirt, groaning, the wet gurgling noise telling her she'd shattered his lungs. Then she stepped to the side and a surge of satisfaction shot through her when she recognized Tino's face in the weak light.

Brody stepped around her and kicked Tino's pistol from his limp hand, then crouched and patted him down all over. "Who else is coming after her," Brody demanded, gripping the thug's chin in his fingers.

Tino tried to jerk his head away. Blood poured out of his nose and mouth and he choked, thrashing weakly.

"Who else, Tino?" she snapped, rage running hot through her veins. This asshole had almost killed her, as well as Brody. She hoped he was in fucking agony right now.

His head rolled a few inches, his blue eyes locking on hers with a mixture of hatred and fear. "Fuck. You," he rasped out, then convulsed.

Brody leaned over him, totally unsympathetic to his plight. "Tell her," he growled.

Too late. Tino had stopped thrashing, his eyes already sliding closed.

While she stood over him Brody checked his carotid pulse, then looked up at her and shook his head.

She was glad he was dead.

"Think he sent anyone else after you?" Brody asked her as he rose, wincing.

"No." At least, she didn't think so. For him this was personal. He'd have wanted to kill her himself. "But we need to get the hell out of here." Because for Tino to have found her apartment—the one she'd rented prior to becoming Eva Gregorivich—it meant someone within the CIA had likely leaked it to him. She was going to dig into that until she had answers, because until the source was found, her life was on the line.

He nodded, stepped up to take her arm as he led her away. "You all right?"

"Yeah. You?"

"I'll feel better once I've got you someplace safe."

With the rush of the hunt over, his words made warmth spread through her body. "Thanks for having my back."

"Any time."

They moved quietly through the cornfield. She was already planning their next move. They had to get out of here before anyone else saw them, then try to disappear while she figured out how to handle this mess. Because somebody had betrayed her. No way he should have been able to find out where her hideout was.

She reached back for Brody's hand when they got to the side of the ditch. He hesitated, scowling, then reluctantly took hers and allowed her to help him descend the steep slope. On the other side she stopped dead when she reached the road.

To her left a truck suddenly appeared at the T in the road and turned the corner. Just as Tino had done, the driver hit the gas and raced straight for them. She automatically dropped to one knee and took aim, ready to shoot the driver.

Brody grabbed her arm, jerking the barrel of the rifle down. "No! It's Wyatt."

Brody stepped past her as the familiar raised truck roared up and screeched to a stop behind Tino's SUV. The headlights shut off then the driver's door shot open and Wyatt exploded out of the cab, racking the pump action of the shotgun in his hands. He stalked toward them, the glare from the other vehicle's headlights showing his deadly expression.

"We're okay," Brody called out, stepping out where Wyatt could see them, motioning to Trinity before raising his hands. He was careful to stay out of the light, in case there were other threats in the area they were unaware of. "They're both dead."

Wyatt's gaze cut to him, then moved from him to Trinity. "Any others?" His voice was tense.

"We don't think so."

Brody hoped she was right.

Wyatt didn't relax his pose, just scanned the immediate area. Brody closed the distance between them, and when he got near enough to see his brother's face up close, he inwardly cursed. Wyatt's nostrils were flared, his jaw clenched tight.

"Hey. We're okay. Look at me," Brody said in a low voice.

Wyatt's hazel eyes finally cut to his, and Brody could see the molten fury mixed with the terror there. Seeing that look from his emotionally distant brother hit him hard. "I'm okay," he repeated quietly, setting a hand on Wyatt's shoulder. No surprise, the muscles there were rock hard, quivering.

Slowly, Wyatt lowered the shotgun. His breathing

was erratic, his posture slowly relaxing. But that terrible mix of rage and fear made Brody's gut clench. His brother had been through a lot of shit and this must have triggered it all over again.

"*Nobody* fucks with my family," Wyatt grated out, his voice low and deadly.

Brody nodded, taken aback by the transformation in his cool, withdrawn brother. The threat was over but Wyatt still looked ready to fucking kill something. "I know, man." He squeezed the solid shoulder. "Thanks for having my back."

Wyatt inhaled and let the breath out slowly, then nodded.

Brody turned back to look at Trinity, who stood frozen by the side of the road, the rifle locked in her grip. He held out a hand, beckoning to her.

She walked toward him, eyeing him and Wyatt. Brody wrapped his arm around her shoulders and pulled her in tight. She wasn't shaky but her breathing was elevated. God, she amazed him. If not for her, he'd likely be lying on the ground bleeding out right now.

"The cops'll be here any minute," Wyatt interrupted.

Brody snapped his attention to him. "What?"

"I called 911 on my work phone on my way here. I knew something bad was going down. You didn't hang up when I called you—I could hear everything that happened from the apartment onward."

Brody reached into his back pocket and pulled out his phone. Sure enough, the call was still connected. He ended it, put the phone away. "How did you find us?"

"Tracked your phone with an app." He transferred the shotgun to one hand, lowered it to his side. "What do you want to do?"

Brody looked at Trinity. When the cops arrived she had to be long gone. If the CIA refused to vouch for her then she could potentially be in a precarious position. "Give me your weapon. You need to get out of here."

Her eyes widened in surprise for a moment before her lips clamped together and she shook her head, holding her rifle out of reach. "No. No way I'm leaving you to deal with this for me."

He stepped forward and snatched it from her, began wiping it for prints. "You have to. Go, quick." His voice was hard, commanding.

He wasn't sure how he was going to explain killing two men or having an unregistered weapon, let alone evidence of her presence left behind. Forensics didn't lie, so it was going to be tricky. He'd have to call DeLuca, try to get help that way before he was forced to lie to the cops about what had happened.

Without wasting time arguing, Brody pushed her toward his brother. "Take her to my place and stay there with her. Don't let her leave." With that he turned and headed back to his truck to await the cops, ready to do whatever it took to protect Trinity.

Chapter THIRTEEN

W yatt's pulse was still beating triple time as he gripped Trinity's upper arm and dragged her toward his truck. He was breathing hard, raw adrenaline coursing through his body.

What. The actual. Fuck.

Whatever the hell Trinity was involved in, it had almost proven deadly tonight. For her *and* his brother.

He clenched his teeth together and bit back all the curses and questions he wanted to bark at her for this. When he'd finally turned onto that road and had seen the body lying on the asphalt, his heart had stopped beating. Even now, having seen that Brody was okay, he was still damn near shaking.

His family was everything to him. *Everything.*

They'd been there for him when no one else had. Through the blackest, bleakest moments of his life that had turned from days into weeks, then into months that had stretched into years. Nobody threatened them or put them at risk, least of all the beautiful woman Brody had for whatever reason risked his life for.

Grits was in the front passenger seat, front paws on the dash, tail wagging as they approached the truck. Wyatt had decided at the last minute to take him along to the VA appointments today and the dog had been a definite hit with the staff and patients there. He might even have the makings of a decent therapy dog.

"Grits. Off," he commanded, snapping his fingers and pointing at the floor.

His pulse was slowing but he was still shaky as hell, queasy with fear and relief. It put him right back to that hellish day in eastern Afghanistan. Every bit of it was wrenchingly vivid in his mind, the sensations careening inside him sharp and fresh as ever. He fought them, afraid he might miss a potential threat still lurking out here in the darkness.

Goddamn it. Goddamn *her*, for doing this to them. "Get in," he growled at her, forcing himself to pry his fingers off her arm. At his deadly tone Grits slunk off the seat and sat in the foot well while Trinity climbed in without a word.

Slamming her door shut, Wyatt stole one last look at his brother, checked around him to make sure everything was okay as it could be, then stalked around to the driver's side and got in. It went against everything in him to abandon Brody right now, and driving the getaway car for her was going to land him in a huge pile of shit if the cops ever found out.

Loyalty to his brother came first. If Brody insisted he take Trinity away, then he would. But he wanted to find out what the hell was going on and just why Brody was willing to stick his neck out so far for her. They'd only met a few damn days ago, so how much could she possibly mean to him? It didn't make any fucking sense.

"How many others are still out there?" he demanded as he started the engine. He was steadier now, but barely in control. Hanging onto his anger by a thread.

Her chin came up. "I don't know, but with Tino gone, I think the coast is clear now." Her voice was calm. Too calm.

The answer wasn't exactly convincing. He did a fast three-point turn and sped back down the road. In the rearview mirror he watched Brody, standing next to Tino's SUV, his shadowy silhouette growing smaller as they drove away.

Wyatt pushed out a hard exhalation and gripped the steering wheel tighter. If Brody got hurt because of this woman, he would tear her apart.

Trinity wanted to argue. She could have broken free of Wyatt's grasp. She could even have ditched both of them and taken off across the cornfield. In this darkness and with their limited mobility, she might have made it, too.

She had done none of those things, for two reasons.

One, Brody was right in that she absolutely needed to be gone by the time the cops arrived. And two, she was going to wait at Brody's because this could turn into a goddamn shit show of bureaucratic bullshit and red tape if she had to get the CIA involved to clear her, and she wasn't about to let Brody wind up facing disciplinary action or worse in an effort to save her ass.

God, it felt wrong to leave him back there to deal with the fallout alone, abandoning him to fend off any more threats should another one materialize. The only thing that helped soothe her conscience was knowing that he was well armed and even better trained. And, as far as she could tell, the threat was over, since Tino and his goon were both dead.

Except whoever had sold her out at the CIA was still alive. She'd lay odds it was her contact for this job, since he'd been the one directly involved with the operation.

Wyatt's jaw was tight as he turned onto a road that would take them toward the highway. She relaxed slightly when she saw the cop cars coming toward them, lights and sirens on. He pulled over to let them pass, then kept going. "Anything happens to him, it's on you," he told her in a cold voice.

I know. "I need your phone."

He frowned, didn't look at her. "For what?"

"I need to call a friend of mine." He gave her another of those distrustful looks and though it went against her self-protective instincts, she realized she needed to give him more. He and his family weren't out to get her, and she'd just put Brody in terrible danger then left him in an awkward situation. "She's married to Brody's commander."

"Why do you want to call her?"

"Just give it to me," she said, holding out her hand.

He shot her a dark glare before pulling his phone out of his pocket and handing it over. She dialed Briar. It went straight to voicemail. Of course she wouldn't pick up if the number wasn't familiar, so she left a message. "Briar, it's Trin. Call me back at this number right away. It's an emergency."

She ended the call and set the phone in her lap, frustration and worry coursing through her. Wyatt had just turned onto the highway when the phone rang. Trinity picked up immediately even though she didn't recognize the number calling. "Hello."

"It's me," Briar said. "What's wrong?"

She let out a sigh of relief. "Long story. Where are you?"

"Just got into D.C. I'm on my way home from the airport."

"Is Matt with you?"

"No, he's still away on an op."

Damn. "I need you to meet me in person as soon as you can." Trinity looked at Wyatt. "I need Brody's address." He aimed another suspicious glance at her, and while she understood his feelings about her, she didn't have time to piss around. "It's for Brody," she said, and he relented and gave it to her.

"You get that?" she asked Briar when Wyatt was done.

"Yeah. What's going on?"

"Rather not say over the phone. How soon can you get there?" She pulled off the wig, sighed and scratched at her head.

"I'm heading there now, so around twenty-five minutes or so, depending on traffic. You need anything?" Her voice was laced with concern.

She knew Briar meant did she need a disguise, IDs, weapons, ammo. Medical care. "No. I'll fill you in when I see you. Bye." She hung up, mind racing. Brody would be talking to the cops right now. She had to have someone intervene on his behalf before the investigation gained momentum. Calling Matt directly might work, but she'd rather talk to Briar about this first, see what her friend thought.

"Why did you call her?" Wyatt asked, his tone curt.

"She and I go way back. We were trained together and she works for the NSA now. If anyone can help us, it's her." Well, her boss. Alex Rycroft.

Wyatt didn't respond, just kept driving. Twenty minutes later they arrived at a brick, ranch-style house in a quiet neighborhood outside Quantico.

He pulled into the driveway, got out and entered a code into the keypad to open the garage door. Then he drove inside, got out and closed the garage door. He eyed her. "You're gonna fix this for Brody, right?"

"Yes, I'm going to find a way to take the heat off

him."

"Come on then," he said, his abrupt tone letting her know she was the last person he wanted here, and that he'd much rather be with his brother right now. He lifted the dog out and carried him inside.

She followed him through a door and into a bright, modern kitchen. Wyatt didn't walk through into the living room to sit on one of the couches. He planted himself at the end of the kitchen counter and stood there glowering at her, feet braced apart, arms folded across his chest. He was even bigger than Brody, would have been downright intimidating if she was the sort to be intimidated, even with Grits there at his feet to soften the image.

Giving him a level stare, she mimicked his stance and waited. They stood there staring at each other through a tense silence and she had to give him credit.

His grim expression never once changed, and he never moved a muscle. Yet she knew if she made one move toward the door, he'd be on her before her hand ever touched the knob. Brody had told him to stay and watch her, and that's exactly what he was doing. She hid a smile, admiring that kind of loyalty.

He pulled his phone out when it buzzed with an incoming text. "She's here," he said to her.

Trinity was already heading for the front door when a brisk knock sounded. Wyatt was on her like a shadow as she stopped in front of it and checked the peephole, Grits right behind him. "It's her." She swung the door open and Briar breezed through. After locking it, Trinity made the introductions.

"Briar, this is Wyatt, Brody's brother. Wyatt, Briar." They nodded at each other, then Briar turned her dark gaze on Trinity, scanning her from head to toe. Her long, dark brown hair was pulled into a low ponytail and she had on black cargo pants and a black long-sleeve T-shirt. Clearly she'd just come back from some kind of op.

"Are you okay?" Briar demanded.

"Yeah."

Frowning, she reached out and pulled Trinity into a tight hug. "You scared me. You've never called in an emergency before."

Trinity squeezed her in return, warmth and affection welling up inside her. They rarely got to see each other, and when they did, it was usually because something had gone wrong. "Well it's kinda been an unprecedented couple of days," she admitted, running a hand through her hair. "Come on, I'll fill you in."

Briar and Wyatt followed her into the living room. Briar sat next to her and Wyatt perched on an easy chair across from them, Grits on his lap, keeping watch while Trinity relayed all the events that had happened over the past few days, leaving out the intimate details about her and Brody.

When she got to the intel leak, Wyatt dragged a hand through his hair. "The CIA? Jesus Christ…" Grits wagged his tail feebly, an almost worried expression on his sweet little face as he sensed the tension in the room.

She ignored Wyatt, her focus on Briar. "I need you to call Rycroft and alert him to what's going on," she finished.

Briar's boss was one of the NSA's most powerful agents. Trinity had met him once before, when she had been on the run. It had given Rycroft the opening he needed to try and recruit her. But Trinity didn't know him well enough to contact him directly, and trusted Briar's discretion about how to handle this. She also knew Rycroft had a big soft spot for Briar.

"What if he says no?" Briar asked.

"Then I'll handle this on my own." Even if she didn't know how yet.

"By doing what?"

"Expose my contact at the CIA." She'd alert the media, leak the story and all the information she had about Salvatori, tell them that a dirty CIA officer had jeopardized the life of a government contractor. It would spread like wildfire. "Someone there had to have leaked intel for Tino and his goon to find my apartment. And if they've leaked info now, then they've done it before. The CIA won't want to deal with the scandal or the dirty officer."

"You do that, they'll target you. You'll have to go on the run."

"If I have to I have to." She'd done it before. "I'm hoping Rycroft will step in. I want him to get in touch with his contacts at the CIA and force them to cover Brody."

"And you," Briar added in a stern tone, a worried frown on her face.

She shrugged. "I knew what the risks were when I signed up for this op. Brody got dragged into this blind. *I* killed Salvatori. *I* killed Tino and his goon. Brody hasn't done anything wrong and I'm not going to let him take the fall for any of this. I'm willing to play hardball with the Agency if necessary, but I'd rather try Rycroft first." It helped to have friends in high places during a situation like this. "Will you call him for me?"

Briar stared at her a moment, measuring her. "All right. But I'm gonna have to bring Matt in on this too."

She'd expected that. "I know."

Briar pulled out her phone and called her boss. After a brief explanation of what was going on, she handed the phone to Trinity.

Trinity answered each of his questions in detail. Normally she'd never reveal the details of her operation to a government agent, but Rycroft had the highest security clearance of anyone she knew. At the moment he was her best hope and she couldn't ask him to get involved unless he knew all the facts.

"Agent Colebrook risked his life and his career to help me," she finished. "My prints will be all over that rifle and there'll be other evidence that I was at the scene tonight. Once they start digging, they're going to uncover all kinds of threads and they'll all lead back to me." They were the freaking CIA, so there was a good chance they could find her if they threw enough money and assets into the hunt, even if she went on the run. "I don't want him to put himself in any further jeopardy by lying for my sake."

"Understood." He paused a moment and she realized she was holding her breath as she awaited his answer. "You tired of running solo contract ops yet?" he asked, his tone level.

The question threw her momentarily. "Maybe." *Come on, say you'll help me.*

He grunted. "All right, I'll make a few calls and do what I can. Given the circumstances the CIA is going to want this whole thing to go away before anyone gets wind of it. But if they've got another dirty agent, we want him or her exposed."

She was counting on that. "What about Agent Colebrook?"

"I'll call DeLuca and we'll handle the cops. I'll call you at this number when I know more."

"Thank you," she said, slumping back into the soft cushions. "I owe you big time."

"Yep," he agreed, a hint of amusement in his voice. "Pretty sure I can think of a way for you to pay it back, too."

She knew what he meant and didn't want to go there yet. Ending the call, she looked at the others. "He's on it. He said he'll call us when he knows more." She pushed to her feet. "I'd like to go take a shower."

Wyatt nodded, his deep-set eyes unreadable as he stroked Grits's head. "Master bedroom's at the end of the hall," he said, jerking his chin to his right.

Briar followed her into the room. The moment she crossed the threshold Trinity smelled Brody's scent. Soap and cologne. It comforted her at the same time as it made her throat tighten.

Briar sat on the foot of the king-size bed, already on the phone to Matt while Trinity headed into the attached bathroom. She stripped and turned on the shower, waited until the water was steaming hot before stepping in and scrubbing herself from head to toe, getting rid of all traces of makeup. The whole time she thought of Brody, wondered what was happening.

Dressed in her scrubs once more, she stepped into the bedroom. Briar watched her. Her friend's dark eyes widened when she saw the bruising on the side of her face. "You lied to me."

"No, I'm okay. Really." She sat beside her. "Looks worse than it is."

Briar set her phone in her lap. "Matt's talking to Rycroft now. They'll do whatever they can to take over the investigation and clear you."

"It's not me I'm worried about, it's Brody."

Briar cocked her head slightly. "That's...different for you. You've only known him what, three days?"

Was it only that many? Felt a helluva lot longer than that. "Doesn't matter. I'm not going to sit back and let him take the fall for any of this. He's worked so hard to rehab his leg after he was shot. I don't want him to lose his chance of rejoining his team because of me."

Those knowing black eyes, a shade or two darker than Brody's, delved into hers. "What happened between you two?"

"Nothing." She stifled the urge to glance away at the lie.

"Bullshit, nothing. Who do you think you're talking to? I know you better than anyone. And so I know there's something going on. You wouldn't do this for him if he didn't matter to you."

"No, there's nothing going on," she insisted. "It's just…he's a good guy. I like and respect him."

She didn't look convinced. "Yeah, he is a good guy."

"I'm not going to let this jeopardize his career or reputation."

Briar didn't answer right away, just watched her with those too-knowing eyes. "If it helps, I can see you two together. You fit. It makes sense."

Trinity sighed, a jagged twinge spearing through her. "Briar. Nothing happened."

She shook her head. "No. He got to you. Didn't he?"

It seemed impossible, but yes. She made a face. "I just don't want to see him in trouble because of me, okay?"

Briar was quiet a long moment, then her eyes widened. "Oh my God, you're terrified."

Trinity snapped her head around to meet her friend's gaze. "I am *not*."

"Yes you are, you're afraid of what he made you feel." A smug grin curved her mouth. "Wow, the black widow of the Valkyries finally met her match. I never thought I'd see the day."

She huffed and pushed to her feet. "Whatever." She was so not talking about this, even with Briar. Her feelings for Brody were complicated and scared the shit out of her. "Let's go wait with Wyatt. He's such great company."

Briar chuckled. "Well he's got good reason not to be your number one fan."

No surprise, he was still in the same chair, manning

his post. He raised a dark eyebrow at them. "Any word?"

"Not yet. What about you?"

"Brody called to say he's at the police station and doesn't know how long he'll be, but not to let you leave."

That offended her pride. "I'm not going anywhere." Not until she'd cleared up this mess for him.

Wyatt didn't answer, just stared at her with those dark, accusing eyes. "You better be worth it."

She didn't know if she was or not but she wasn't leaving until she fixed this and saw Brody again.

They all looked at Briar when her phone rang. She checked the display and announced, "It's Rycroft," before answering.

Trinity was aware of her pulse accelerating as she watched Briar, listening to her side of the conversation and trying to decipher what was going on. A minute later, Briar hung up. "He says it's being taken care of. The police will release Brody soon."

Good. That was good. "What about the rest?"

"He said it's being handled and that's all we need to know." Translated into layman's terms, that meant he wasn't going to tell them what he did know because the less they knew, the better.

"I owe him." So much, she wasn't sure she could ever make it up to him. She'd never forget what Brody had done for her, all the feelings he'd awoken in her.

"You know he wants to recruit you," Briar said. "He's wanted you on his team since before I joined."

"I know."

"Will you think about it?"

Trinity didn't answer, feeling too exposed in front of Wyatt. He already knew too much and she didn't blame him for continuing to watch her like a bug under a microscope. But yeah, she'd think about it. She didn't want to continue down this path anymore. She wanted to be free to have a life again, maybe someone to share it with one day.

Maybe Brody.

A quiet ringtone went off. Wyatt put his phone to his ear. "Hey." He listened to whoever it was, she hoped Brody, all the while watching her. "Yeah, she's still here. According to your commander's wife, everything's being handled. That true?" Whatever he said must have verified that, because Wyatt's tense posture eased. "Okay. See you soon." He hung up, his gaze still pinning her. "He's on his way."

"That's my cue to leave," Briar said with a wry edge to her voice. She looked at Trinity, raised an eyebrow. "Walk me to the door?"

Feeling Wyatt's stare following her, Trinity accompanied Briar to the front door. "Thanks for coming and helping me out. I appreciate it."

Briar snorted softly and shook her head. "I'd do whatever it took to help you or Georgia, and you know it. Just like I know you would do the same for me."

Trinity nodded. "Yeah, I would."

Briar reached for her and Trinity wrapped her arms around her friend. "Will you be going back to London now?" she asked against Trinity's hair.

"Tomorrow." She didn't want to think about that yet because she had unfinished business with Brody. Even if the threat was officially over, the way she felt about him scared her to death.

She had no reference point for this, no protocol to fall back on that would help her deal with it or make a decision about what to do. The Valkyrie cadre was supposed to have trained the desire for this kind of emotional attachment to a man out of her for good. "Maybe next time I'm in town we could get together and actually spend time having fun." Trinity squeezed her harder, hating to let her go.

"I'd love that." Pulling back, Briar searched her eyes. "I know how you feel about wanting to leave, and I know we don't trust easily, especially men, but Brody really is a good guy. Don't push him away because you're afraid of what will happen. You'll regret it if you do."

She forced a smile. How ironic to be on the receiving end of that advice, given that Trinity was six years older and had always played the role of mother figure to her fellow Valkyries. "Thanks for the words of wisdom, young padawan."

"Hey, I've been there," she said with a grin. "You may be way more experienced than me when it comes to men, but I've got a leg up on you in terms of relationship experience. I was scared to death at first but letting Matt in was the best decision I ever made." She set a hand on Trinity's shoulder. "You've done enough. It's time to put the past behind you and go after what you want. You deserve to be happy."

The words made her throat tighten. For as long as she could remember she'd suppressed her own needs and wants, maybe because part of her felt that she didn't deserve anything more. Now that she'd met Brody, however, she wanted more. She just wasn't sure if she could have it. "Thanks. Love you."

"Love you back." Briar hugged her one more time, then was gone.

Trinity closed the door and stood there alone in the foyer with butterflies swirling in her stomach. Brody would be home soon. Their time together had been short but intense and the bottom line was, she trusted him. When she left tomorrow, she at least wanted to take the memory of him with her, even if it meant leaving a part of her heart behind.

Much as it scared her, this time she was going to take what she wanted and make the most of their last night together.

Chapter FOURTEEN

Anticipation hummed through Brody as he parked the rental car in his driveway and stared at his house. All because Trinity was waiting for him inside.

He still couldn't believe the strings she'd managed to pull in such a short time, and that he'd been allowed to go. His truck had been turned over for further investigation by a government agency, he was guessing the NSA.

During their brief phone conversations Rycroft and DeLuca hadn't told him the details, but Brody had been released with the promise to cooperate with the NSA in the upcoming investigation. He suspected Rycroft would handle this personally, in part to expose the dirty officer, and also to keep tabs on the kinds of off-the-books ops the CIA had going on.

He was just glad he'd been allowed to go, and that Trinity was being looked after by someone he trusted. He and Wyatt weren't as close now as they'd once been but there was an unbreakable bond between him and all his siblings. No matter what, they would always have each other's backs.

On his way to the front door, his heartbeat picked up. Trinity planned to leave tomorrow night but he was going to do everything in his power to try and change her mind. He wanted more time together, wanted to break through her outer shell and see where things went between them. If she'd let him in, he thought they had a shot at something awesome.

Right now there was only one thing he wanted. As soon as he could get rid of his brother, Brody was getting Trinity naked and into his bed.

He didn't want to think about her running into that cornfield earlier, hunting down Tino. He *definitely* didn't want to think about the kit the cops had found in the back of Tino's SUV. Scalpels, other torture tools, a plastic sheet, bleach, restraints and condoms. If that evil son of a bitch had taken Trinity, she'd have suffered unimaginable horrors before he killed her. Brody was glad the bastard was dead.

He found her and Wyatt in the family room. Trinity gave him a warm smile full of relief, the wig she'd been wearing was gone and her face scrubbed clean of all the makeup she'd put on earlier.

She looked beautiful and kissable. The urge to rush over and grab her was so strong he had to force himself to stop where he was.

Wyatt pushed to his feet, holding Grits in one arm, scanning Brody with a critical eye while Trinity stood but didn't approach him. "Hi," she said.

"Hi." Her gaze stroked over him like a caress, heating his blood as he stood there.

"You okay?" Wyatt asked gruffly.

"Yeah, I'm good. Thanks for everything."

His brother grunted and shot a sideways glance at

Trinity before looking back at him. "You need anything else?"

"No. You heading home now?" He probably was being a dick, to kick his brother out after all Wyatt had done for him tonight, but he had limited time left with Trinity and he didn't want to waste a moment of it.

"Guess so," he said, huffing out a dry laugh. He turned his attention to Trinity. "Will I see you again?"

"I don't think so."

"Well, it's been interesting. You take care."

"You too."

Brody walked him out to the garage. Wyatt put Grits in the passenger seat, shut the door then stopped and turned to face him. "You care about her."

He nodded.

"A lot."

It surprised him, how much she'd gotten to him in such a short amount of time, but that didn't change his feelings and he didn't see the point in denying them. "Yes."

Wyatt studied him for a few seconds. "Is she worth it?"

He didn't even hesitate. "Yeah."

A grudging smile pulled at that hard mouth. "Okay then. In that case, you should know she was ready to go to the mat for you."

Brody frowned. "How do you mean?"

"If Rycroft didn't help clear you, she was going to leak her story and sources to the press."

Dread coiled in his stomach. "She would have been blacklisted." It would have put her in further danger. Someone in the CIA might even have issued a kill order for her.

Wyatt nodded. "I know. She was ready to do it anyway, prepared to go on the run if she had to, as long as you were cleared first. Only reason I know is because

she had to explain everything to her friend and I
wouldn't let her out of my sight for that part so I got to
overhear everything."

Ah, hell. Brody absorbed the enormity of that, her
willingness to sacrifice herself for him. She had the
aloof, untouchable façade down to an art, but there was
way more to her and her actions hit him square in the
heart.

"Call me if you need anything," Wyatt said.

"I will. Thanks, man." He clapped him on the
shoulder, stood there until Wyatt's taillights disappeared
around the corner, and closed the garage door.

His body was on heightened alert as he walked back
into the kitchen. Trinity was standing there next to the
counter, waiting for him, the loose hospital scrubs
disguising the curves he was itching to explore with his
hands and mouth. He couldn't believe she'd been willing
to go to such lengths to protect him. How was he
supposed to let her go after this?

"Rycroft said everything was being taken care of,"
she said.

"Seems that way. You've got powerful friends."

"Briar sweet talked him for me." She let her gaze
travel over the length of his body with pure female
appreciation, then came back up to meet his, increasing
the heat and hunger spreading inside him. She walked
toward him, her movements sinuous, everything about
her screaming sex. "How's your leg?"

"Still attached." Throbbed like a damn toothache
but he'd be damned if it stopped him from enjoying her
to the fullest. The ache in his cock helped distract him
from it anyway.

She stopped directly in front of him, a mere breath
of air separating them, and set a hand on the side of his
face. The heat of her body reached out to him, her clean,
soapy scent. "Why did you do it?" she asked softly.

"Why did you let me run and stay behind to face the consequences for me?"

He slid his hands into her hair, fingers rubbing against her scalp. At the time he hadn't thought about it much, he'd just been going with instinct. Now he realized it was because she meant something to him. "It was the only thing I could do to protect you."

Her eyes darkened as he kept caressing her. "If Rycroft hadn't stepped in, you could've lost everything. Your job, your security clearance. Your reputation. So why risk it all?" She sounded bewildered.

"Because you're worth it."

Surprise filled her gaze, then a split second of naked vulnerability that made his heart clench. "You don't know that," she whispered.

"Yes I do." But words weren't going to convince her what he felt for her. Actions might though.

Needing to touch her, to ease this craving she caused in him, he tipped her face up and bent to brush his lips against the corner of her mouth. Her hands flew to his shoulders, gripping tight, her sharply indrawn breath sending a streak of fire through his gut. "I want you so damn bad." His entire body was rigid with need.

In answer she turned her lips to his, deepened the kiss.

Brody eased back, satisfaction roaring inside him when she made a sound of protest and tried to pull him back. Except he didn't want her doing this out of a sense of obligation. This had to be as authentic for her as it was for him, or he would rather walk away right now, even if it would damn near kill him.

Trinity gazed up at him, her expression calm but her eyes blazed with raw yearning. Much as he wanted to devour her, this wasn't just physical for him.

It was about showing her that she mattered to him, about showing her how good they would be together if she just gave them the chance. He could practically feel her locking armor around her heart, maybe in an attempt to minimize the emotional impact of what was coming.

No way, sweetheart. Not this time.

He held her gaze, let the tension build. The need to break through that barrier was overpowering, but so was the need to imprint himself on her forever. She might have seduced men in the past on ops, but in reality she'd been the one being used. That all stopped now.

He was going to show her how good sex could be with the right partner, with a man who cared about her and was willing to put her needs before his own.

Staring into her eyes, a flicker of uncertainty formed there, the beginnings of doubt, and it tugged at him. She was thinking way too hard.

"Give me tonight," he murmured, cradling the back of her head in his hands. It wasn't as much as he wanted, but it was probably all he'd get. For now. Because he had no intention of letting her go without a fight.

After a moment she gave a slight nod, whispered, "Yes."

It was enough.

Brody let out a low groan and crushed his lips to hers. She gasped and grabbed hold of his shoulders, her fingers digging into his muscles.

Knowing she wanted him just as bad as he wanted her hit him like a double shot of whiskey.

He plunged his tongue into her mouth, tasting her, every sense alive, the burning need to possess her lashing at him. Everything about her was unexpected, a challenge. He wanted to strip her naked and take right here but held back, because he wanted her to remember this as the best she'd ever had. That *he* was the best she'd *ever* have.

Determined to prove it, he locked his arms around her and lifted her against the wall, pinning her there with his weight. Eventually she might come back to him once she got out of her own way. He wasn't willing to leave that to chance.

She might be planning to walk away tomorrow, but by God, he would make sure she never forgot him when she did.

Chapter FIFTEEN

Trinity's heart knocked against her ribs so hard she was sure Brody must have heard it. The weight and heat of his hard body pressed to hers filled her with a yearning so intense she could barely breathe.

She shouldn't do this. Sleeping with him was going to make it hurt like hell when she left tomorrow, but she refused to deny herself the chance to experience this with him. Just once, she wanted something real. A beautiful moment she could actually remember later on, and not force herself to block.

She leaned into his body, relishing his strength, the feel of his mouth on hers, the desperate grip of his hands as he held her to the wall. Being pinned should have made her feel trapped, awakened her fighting instincts. Instead it only fueled the hunger burning inside her and made her want to surrender to him.

It might be crazy to want that given they barely knew each other, but she trusted him on the deepest level and he was already under her skin. He'd put himself in harm's way to protect her, had been willing to face the fallout tonight to make sure she got clear. Now she wanted him to unleash the inner sensuality she'd withheld from everyone else, free her of the burden of always having to be in control.

Losing control was her worst fear, yet she wanted to do just that with Brody.

He rocked his hips against hers, rubbing the rigid length of his erection along her covered mound. Jolts of pleasure shot through her, dragging a needy moan from her throat.

Her breasts felt swollen and heavy, the throb between her legs growing with each stroke of his tongue, each motion of his hips. She wanted him naked, to feel him skin to skin.

He slid one hand to the back of her head, gripped her hair as his other arm banded around her hips and he pulled her free of the wall. She wrapped her arms and legs around him, a moment of worry breaking through the haze of passion as she thought about his injured leg.

"I can walk," she told him breathlessly.

"No," he muttered. "Don't wanna let you go even for a second." He fused their mouths together and carried her down the hall.

His words all but melted her. It was ridiculously romantic, tugging at a part of her heart that she'd long denied. She was sure the additional weight hurt him but he didn't complain, didn't ease his grip until they reached his bedroom and he laid her down on the comforter.

Before she could reach for him he was pulling the scrub top off her. She sat up and raised her arms to help him. A thrill sizzled through her at the way his gaze heated when it fastened on her breasts straining in the bra she'd found at the costume shop. Lowering her hand, she undid the front clasp, slowly removed the material.

When her breasts spilled free he groaned and cupped them in his big hands, squeezing and kneading gently, the slight roughness of the calluses on his palms adding another layer of sensation.

Her breasts ached, the nipples hard and demanding attention. She gripped the back of his head as he ran his thumbs over them, making her shiver. Sparks of sensation flew outward from his touch, shooting down to coil between her thighs. She was already wet for him, needing him to slide into her and take away the emptiness.

It had been so long since she'd done this for any kind of pleasure, she wasn't even sure if her body remembered what to do. He'd awakened a part of her that she'd suppressed for too long and now she couldn't shut it off. There might be no future for them but she couldn't resist him and since this was only for one night and she'd never see him again she was determined to enjoy this. Even if part of her was trying to convince her to stay.

He kissed his way down her neck, pausing to run his tongue over her pulse point. She tipped her head back and held on, arching her spine as he moved down to her sensitive breasts. The moment his mouth closed over a tight nipple pleasure forked through her, ripping a whimper from her throat.

She closed her eyes, allowed herself to get lost in the delicious sensation, her arousal heightened by the possessive yet tender way he handled her. With everyone else she'd faked this, acting the part while remaining coldly detached.

She wasn't acting now.

Trinity writhed as he licked and sucked her nipple. She was barely aware of him pulling her shoes and the scrub bottoms off.

He swept his hand over the silver-dollar-sized tat on the side of her left hip. The mark of the Valkyrie, designed by her and Briar and Georgia after they'd graduated. A black crow with a sword clutched in its talons, and the word *Valkyrja* written inside a stylized scroll below it.

"Valkyrie," he murmured, his deep voice stroking through her in another caress.

Then his gaze moved over her belly and a jolt of awareness intruded, penetrating through the arousal. She'd learned long ago not to let her hysterectomy scar bother her but Brody wasn't like the other men she'd been with. He held the power to hurt her far more than anyone ever had.

Her muscles stiffened when his gaze stopped on the thin scar, a frown pulling at his forehead as he slid his fingertips over it. Then he looked up at her and the quiet disbelief and rage confirmed he understood what it meant.

The risk of pregnancy wasn't acceptable for someone with her job description, or so they'd made her believe. Shortly after her trainer had introduced her to the brutal reality of the threat she faced in the field, she'd been scheduled for a hysterectomy. At the time it had seemed logical. A permanent, practical solution for birth control that would prevent what would be an extreme inconvenience in her line of work.

Back then, it hadn't bothered her much. It wasn't until she'd hit her twenties that she realized the enormity of what had been taken from her. The finality of it.

But she didn't want to think about that right now, and she sure as hell didn't want his pity. "It was a long time ago," she whispered. "And I don't want you to stop."

Brody leaned up to take her mouth in a scorching kiss, his hand splayed protectively over her lower abdomen. When her head began to swim he lowered his head to her other nipple and this time the pleasure streaked hotter, sharper. The ache between her legs was nearly unbearable and she couldn't wait another moment to get him naked.

A sense of urgency gripping her, she stripped off his shirt and ran her hands appreciatively over all that hard muscle. He had a bulldog tat with the letters USMC on his right shoulder, and from the thin leather cord around his neck dangled a 7.62 mm round. His hog's tooth—the coveted symbol of his status as a Marine scout-sniper.

Stroking her fingertips over it, she trailed her hands lower before following her touch with her mouth. His clean, masculine scent drove her crazy, made her want to rub all over him to cover herself in it.

Strong hands cupped her head, tipping her face up. His mouth crashed down on hers. The kiss was frantic, greedy, a tangle of tongues and lips, tiny nips that stoked the fires impossibly higher.

Her hands went to his belt buckle. He didn't help, didn't stop kissing her as she undid it, took off his boots and peeled his jeans over his hips. He rolled to the side to shuck them off, then his underwear.

His cock jutted out from his abdomen, thick and swollen and she couldn't wait to feel it inside her, but when she slipped a hand down to curl around him, he stopped her and pushed her back on the sheets. "Lie still," he ordered in a husky murmur that made her toes curl.

His big hands pressed against her shoulders, reinforcing his command. She complied, because she trusted him, and knew that he wouldn't use this to manipulate her or exploit this vulnerability.

Heart racing, she tried to relax, dying for more. Brody set a hand on either side of her head and leaned over her, caging her in, making her feel protected, wanted. The way he looked into her eyes shook her, took this to a whole new level of intimacy. It pierced her to her soul.

He kissed her gently now, once, twice, then layered kisses and gentle licks down the side of her neck, pausing to tease her tingling nipples before sweeping over her stomach. Her muscles clenched, her thighs tightening in anticipation of what was coming.

But he didn't push a hand between her legs, didn't rush. Instead, he smoothed his palms over her stomach and hips, down her thighs, trailing his fingertips over the sensitive insides on the way back up. Over and over, all the while licking and kissing her lower belly until she was so wet and desperate she was squirming.

His fingers brushed the top of her mound, gliding through the strip of trimmed hair there, making each nerve ending sizzle. She sucked in a breath and grabbed his shoulders, sinking her fingers into his muscles. He was so strong yet tender with her, and the care he took to arouse her fully made her heart turn over.

Desperate for relief but afraid to speak in case it broke the spell, she bit her lower lip and watched through heavy-lidded eyes as he dragged those skilled fingers down the center of her folds, his touch light as a breath.

She groaned and rolled her hips, silently pleading for more. Every man she'd ever been with had taken, only concerned with their own pleasure. Brody, on the other hand, was a giver. It was a new, incredible experience.

The warm stroke of his tongue moved lower, stopping just short of his teasing fingers as he brushed them against her most sensitive flesh. Then he dipped between her folds to slip down and caress her entrance, gathering wetness before slowly, torturously moving back to her throbbing clit.

She hissed in a breath as his fingertip made contact with the hard nub, her entire body shaking from the lash of pleasure. Her eyes slid closed, too heavy to keep open, and he rewarded the gesture of surrender with slick, tender swirls and spirals right where she needed them.

A long, liquid moan spilled out of her and her legs began to quiver, heat gathering deep in her core as the release she craved began to gather already.

With a sound of approval Brody trailed his mouth lower, gliding his fingers down to press two inside her. The warmth of his breath touched her aching flesh, then the velvet stroke of his tongue took her breath away.

Her body moved in an uncontrollable wave, her hands tunneling in his hair to hold him closer. God, it was so intense and he was so damn giving, so patient.

He licked and sucked her clit until she whispered his name in a plea for release, then he curled his fingers and began stroking at the sweet spot inside her that no man had ever taken the time to locate, let alone arouse.

God...

Sensation burst through her in waves of pleasure, the heat coiling tighter and tighter. She pushed against his mouth, reaching for the orgasm waiting for her, just out of her grasp.

He stopped, pulled his mouth away.

No!

Her eyes snapped open in shock. Brody stared up at her from between her legs, his lips glistening in the midst of that dark stubble. He continued stroking his fingers inside her in lazy caresses, making her shiver all over as liquid pleasure streaked through her veins.

And the look in his eyes... The raw hunger there stole her breath, made her unable to voice the plea that had been waiting on her tongue.

A second after she'd made eye contact he lowered his head and resumed what he'd been doing. She melted back against the covers, lost in the pleasure he was giving her so freely. Then he dragged the pads of his fingers over that sweet ache inside her and she couldn't take it anymore.

"Please make me come," she begged, her voice breathy, unrecognizable. She didn't care that she was pleading and spread out helpless beneath him, she needed him to give her the release she was dying for.

Brody growled low in his throat, gave her one last lingering lick before surging to his knees and rolling on a condom he'd pulled from his wallet. She didn't even have time to appreciate the sight of his thick, hard cock before he was moving between her thighs.

Wrapping her legs around his, she pulled his head down to kiss him. She felt the pressure of him against her opening, his tongue gliding along hers as he eased forward, his weight balanced on one arm.

Pressure and heat suffused her as he pushed deeper. God, he was so thick, filling her completely, the sensation robbing her of breath.

He stroked over that sweet spot inside her at the same time he reached between them and rubbed her clit. Trinity moaned into his mouth and fought to get closer, her entire body shaking with need. His hips flexed as he buried himself inside her, his low groan swallowed up by their kiss.

Easing his head back, he stared into her eyes as he began to move, giving her slow, steady thrusts as he caressed her clit.

Too much.

She squeezed her eyes shut, a cry of need and joy spilling free as she neared the peak. She rocked into his thrusts, opened her thighs wider so he could caress every delicate nerve ending that shivered beneath his fingertip.

Her muscles clenched around him, holding him tight inside her as the orgasm hit, blasting pleasure out to every part of her. She distantly heard her wild moans of release filling the room, clung to him while he groaned and thrust harder, dropping his head to her shoulder.

The orgasm was only beginning to ebb as she ran her hands over his damp shoulders and over his back. Brody moaned and pumped harder, faster, and he swelled even thicker inside her.

She pressed her lips to his temple, gripped the back of his neck and dug her heels into his taut ass. "I want to feel you come for me."

He shuddered at her words. "Trin," he gasped out, then thrust deep and arched, eyes squeezed closed, teeth bared as he groaned out his release.

She gathered him close, savoring the feel of his weight pressing her down, blanketing her with warmth and security. He'd given her the best sex of her life but it had felt far more intimate than that. He'd made love to her.

The knowledge made her throat tighten.

Not wanting to think about it, she focused on each sensation as they lay entwined, their hearts beating together. Still buried inside her, Brody sighed and nestled closer, resting his face in the curve of her neck, his arms sliding beneath her back to hold her tight. Her heart clenched, a sweet ache forming beneath her ribs as she wrapped her arms around him and simply held on.

She'd never felt this close to anyone. Ever.

She swallowed, fighting the onslaught of emotion as a lump formed in her throat. God, she liked this way too much.

He made her want things that had always been forbidden to her before, things she'd never let herself imagine having. A relationship with a man she wanted and trusted. Someone to come home to at night, a man strong enough to lean on when things got hard. A lasting partnership.

Everything in her told her he was that person. And that scared the hell out of her. She wasn't normal. Didn't know how to make a relationship work, even if she wanted to.

Brody stirred and groaned softly as he withdrew and rolled off her. "Be right back," he murmured, pausing to drop a tender kiss to her lips before going into the bathroom. A minute later he returned, tugging the covers over them as he slid in beside her.

Though self-preservation told her to get up and put some distance between them, she couldn't. Not after what they'd just shared. He gathered her in his arms and she was all too content to cuddle against his muscular chest. She was going to miss this—miss him—so much.

She slid her right hand down to his thigh, caressed the surgical scars there. "How's your leg?" she whispered, instinctively wanting to lighten the mood.

"What leg," he said, a smile in his voice. He kissed the top of her head then leaned back a little to look into her eyes. He cupped her cheek, rubbed his thumb gently over her skin, that chocolate-brown gaze seeing straight into her soul. "You sure about flying out tomorrow?"

Her stomach tightened and she lowered her gaze. "Yeah. I need to get back." To her solitary, gray existence in London where she wouldn't dream impossible dreams and pine for something she could never have. Because she was too afraid to stay and risk her heart.

He didn't say anything, didn't show any disappointment or anger. Instead, he gathered her close, tucked her head beneath his chin and stroked her hair, making her insides quake. "Stay with me. At least a few more days, and we can see how things go."

The request sent twin arrows of pain and longing

through her. She hesitated a moment before answering, knowing she had to be honest but unable to admit how afraid she was. "I can't."

"Just think about it," he coaxed, hugging her tight. "Gotta warn you, though. By tomorrow night I plan to do everything in my power to make sure you'll never be able to forget me."

Forget him? Not possible. The man stole more pieces of her heart with every minute she stayed in his arms. By the time her flight left tomorrow, there might be nothing left.

Even that threat wasn't enough to make her climb out of his bed.

This time was for her. Something to carry with her forever. She wasn't giving it up for anything.

Snuggled safe and secure in his embrace, Trinity closed her eyes and prayed she'd be strong enough to leave him when the time came.

Chapter SIXTEEN

The hard knot of dread in the pit of Trinity's stomach wound tighter with each mile they came closer to the airport. Every cell in her body was attuned to Brody as he drove the rental car, and she was vividly aware of how fast their remaining minutes together were ticking past.

The last sixteen hours had been the most incredible of her life.

He'd woken her before dawn with erotic caresses over her naked skin, his lips and tongue teasing every sensitive spot until she'd begged him for release. Afterward they'd fallen back to sleep. When she'd dragged herself out of bed a few hours later for a shower, he'd climbed in with her, spending endless minutes gliding his soapy hands over her wet body.

He'd fed her, then coaxed her back into bed and she'd been powerless to resist even though she knew she should start distancing herself from him. They'd spent the entire day in bed together, cuddling and talking, something she'd never done with anyone—something she'd never *wanted* to do—and now….

She stole a sideways glance at him, hoping her inner turmoil didn't show. She'd been careful to hide it, but all day long it had been getting worse.

All last night and throughout the day she'd continually tried to convince herself that their attraction was simply chemical, but that was a total lie. Against all odds she'd let him into her heart and now there was no getting him out.

He'd stepped up to help her when she'd been a total stranger, had gone above and beyond by giving her a safe place to hide at his family home and risking his life to help her. She'd seen him with his dad and brother, in his most private and intimate space.

He'd been so protective of her, so caring and tender last night and she felt so comfortable around him. The thought of getting on the plane and flying across the Atlantic and never seeing him again gutted her.

Give me tonight.

She'd been more than willing to give him that. Then he'd asked her to stay and it scared her how much she wanted to, because one night wasn't enough for her anymore. Not with him.

The shitty part was, she didn't see how they could make a relationship work. His life was here in Virginia and she was based out of London. He had deep roots here. A family that loved him. He would hopefully return to the job he loved in a few months once his leg healed.

She, on the other hand, had no roots. Nothing to anchor her anywhere, except her place in London, which was the closest thing she'd ever had to a real home. She didn't even know what she wanted to do with her life after this, except that she was done with taking contract hits.

No matter how many monsters she killed, there would always be more. Last night with Brody and Briar's parting words kept haunting her.

She *did* deserve to be happy after all she'd done for the government and all they'd taken from her. She just didn't know what that happy life looked like yet, or how to go about getting it. What she needed most right now was space, some time alone to think everything through.

"Traffic's a lot worse than I thought it would be," Brody commented in a neutral voice as he took the exit to the airport. "You're not gonna have much time to get through security and to your gate."

"It's okay, I don't like hanging around in airports anyway. I always try to get there as late as I can." Her voice sounded calm, unaffected, when in reality it felt like her chest was slowly constricting.

He was quiet a moment before glancing at her. "Can I call you after you get back?"

The question took her aback. She knew it was probably smarter, kinder for her to just cut all ties with him, make a clean cut rather than a jagged one. She wasn't selfless enough for that though. "Of course you can call me."

"Yeah? You gonna answer?" he asked in a wry tone.

She grinned. He knew her so well already. Warmth spread through her. "I'll answer."

"You ever gonna call me though?" he asked.

That one was harder. She squeezed her hands together in her lap. "I'm not the best person for staying in touch. Just ask Briar." She'd spent a lifetime avoiding close relationships because her job demanded it, and because it had been ingrained into her. "But I'll try."

The flash of hurt she saw on his face before he looked away sliced at her insides. God, that had sounded so cold after what they'd shared, but she needed to make it clear to him that there was no future for them. She would not string him along or give him false hopes. He needed to know where they stood. He belonged here, and she…

Well, she didn't know where she belonged yet.

Her chaotic emotions unsettled her. She'd never been in this situation before, had never wanted anyone this badly, and didn't know how to handle it. Her brain and heart were at war, each side giving compelling arguments for why it was the right choice. Stay open to him and see where things went—if they went anywhere at all—or sever ties now and move on, and in time she'd forget him.

Except that deep down she'd never forget him, no matter what she did or how far she ran. She would never get over him, and knowing that scared her almost as much as losing her heart to him. Dammit, she *was* good enough to have a normal life, to fall in love and finally stop running from everyone. Especially herself.

Brody took the turnoff to the short-term parking garage. "Oh no, you can just drop me off out front," she said, an unfamiliar panicky sensation swirling in her gut. She was torn between the urge to jump out of the car and run and tell him to keep driving, past the airport, all the way back to his place.

"Can't wait to get rid of me, huh?" His tone was light but she sensed the hurt and disappointment beneath it.

She only wanted to escape because each minute he prolonged the inevitable just made it worse. Once she got out of this car, once she got away from him, she'd be able to breathe again. Except just the thought of walking away made it feel like her heart was cracking in two.

Ignoring her request, he entered the parking garage and found a spot near the elevators. When he turned off the engine and glanced over at her, she steeled herself.

"Look. I don't want to make this any harder than it already is."

"I do."

She blinked at his response, her mouth snapping shut.

"If you think I'm gonna make it easy for you to just brush me off and walk away, think again." With that he got out of the car and came around to open her door before she could climb out. His warm, chocolate-brown eyes held hers and that bone deep connection locked into place again.

Then he took her hand and the moment their fingers touched, electricity sizzled over her palm and up her arm. She stood there unmoving, gazing up at him. For the life of her she couldn't pull away.

"I'm really glad you broke into my commander's house the other night," he said, a grin tugging at his sexy mouth.

She laughed softly, the tension inside her easing a fraction even as the ache intensified. "Me too."

"You sure about this?"

"Yes."

He kissed her softly and laced his fingers through hers, his tone resigned. "Come on then."

God, she was dreading this. A public goodbye in front of whoever happened to be standing at the check-in counter? She just prayed her acting skills held up long enough for him not to see her fall apart. Which she was pretty sure she would do once she got through security and could find a bathroom to hide in.

His fingers were warm and strong around hers as they walked toward the terminal. With each step closer to the building her heartbeat accelerated, the knot in her stomach cinching tighter. Her emotions were all over the place, a chaotic torrent inside her. She wanted to pull away and she wanted to push closer. She wanted to stay and she wanted to escape.

God, just let me get through security without breaking down.

They reached the automatic doors at the front of the international terminal. The moment they whooshed open and she saw the lines of travelers gathered in front of the check-in counters, the finality of it hit her.

She squeezed Brody's hand tighter, tried her damnedest not to tear up. He glanced at her, returned the pressure and brought her hand to his lips, pressing a warm kiss to the back of it.

Her throat tightened and she had to swallow to ease the restriction. She felt half numb as she headed for the desk marking her airline, just wanted this to be over. The initial walking away was going to be the hardest part. Once she got through that, time and distance would help her get through this.

She walked right up to the first class check-in and stopped. *Do it now. Make a clean cut and walk away.*

Turning to Brody, she gazed up at him and the goodbye she'd prepared wouldn't come. How had he come to mean so much to her in so little time? It didn't make sense. This wasn't like her. She lived in a world of black and white and in just a few short days he'd turned everything gray. What the hell was wrong with her?

"Well," she began, bracing herself for the coming pain. "Thanks again, for everything." For protecting her. For making her feel respected, cared about, and even…loved.

He nodded, regret and longing in his eyes. "Anytime."

"I'll text you once I land to let you know I got there."

"I'd appreciate that." Then his expression sobered even more and it felt like he was looking inside her as he spoke, his eyes searching hers. "Remember, I'm here if you need me."

"I will." She couldn't look away, was afraid to touch him because for the first time in memory she was on the verge of tears.

Come with me, she almost blurted, barely biting the words back in time, even though the idea was beyond crazy. His life was here and he had to stay put during the duration of the NSA investigation. She had loose ends to tie up in London, and lots to think about.

And if she stayed here any longer, she'd fall completely, utterly in love with him.

Go. Now. Before you do something stupid. "Bye," she murmured, and leaned up to press her lips to his because she couldn't help herself.

But she should have known Brody wouldn't let it go at that.

"Don't go," he said, capturing her face between his hands.

Pain twisted inside her. "I have to," she whispered, her voice catching.

"No you don't."

She grabbed his wrists, ready to push his hands away. "Yes, I do."

He kissed her, slow and deep and tender, right out in the open in front of anyone who cared to watch.

And she let him. Didn't even think about pulling away.

When he finally released her, her knees were weak and she had to fight to keep from reaching for him. "If you change your mind about us, you know where to find me."

The lump in her throat felt like it had swelled to the size of a damn baseball. She forced a tight smile, even though she knew it didn't reach her eyes. "Bye, Brody."

It went against every instinct to turn and walk away. She held her back ramrod straight as she stood at the counter and handed over her fake passport to the woman there, trying her best to ignore Brody, and failing miserably. She could feel the weight of his stare on her, felt her resolve slip another notch.

When the woman returned her boarding pass, a sense of relief washed through her. Too late now. The decision had been made.

Bracing herself, she looked over her shoulder and met Brody's gaze. Giving him a small smile, she lifted a hand in farewell, the ache of tears burning the back of her throat when he did the same. He made her feel safe, cherished. Knowing she was about to walk away forever was almost too much to bear.

You're making it worse. Go.

She forced herself to turn away and head for the security lineup. When she glanced back to look for him a minute later, he was gone.

As a cold emptiness spread through her, she felt a sharp stab of pain in her chest and finally knew what a broken heart felt like.

****

Brody needed to get drunk. As soon as possible. It was the only way to escape the pain for tonight.

He could drive back to the Shenandoah before getting shitfaced but he didn't feel like being interrogated by his dad and Wyatt. He'd rather drown his sorrows in private, at his own place. Which would only remind him of her. And when he crawled into bed tonight his sheets would still smell like her.

Dammit…

Heaving a sigh, he headed back toward his rental car. It hurt like hell to let her go but he had no other choice. She'd made it clear that last night was a one-time thing and she was clearly anxious to get back to London.

He worried about her though. She might be the strongest woman he'd ever met but he knew she must be lonely. There was so much life in her, so much passion, he couldn't handle thinking of her living the kind of bleak existence she had up to now. And part of him feared that if she continued that life, sooner or later it would catch up with her.

Sooner or later, someone better than her would catch her and end her life. Jesus, even thinking it made him sick to his stomach.

He stopped as a bus of tourists poured out onto the sidewalk and blocked his path, making him miss the light. It didn't surprise him that Trinity had pulled away from him emotionally the moment they'd gotten into the car tonight. He wasn't sure what he'd been hoping for, but the way she'd left filled him with bitter disappointment. She'd text him when she landed in London, but he already knew how this was going to play out after that.

He'd be the one to reach out, try to maintain some sort of contact. She'd never call him. Whether it was because she just wasn't as into him as he'd hoped, or whether it was to protect herself from what he'd made her feel, he didn't know. And it didn't matter. Bottom line, as far as she was concerned, they were done.

It felt like his chest was filled with lead as he walked to the car. This sucked ass and it fucking hurt worse than when he'd been shot. He didn't even have his job to keep him busy and give him something else to focus on. The thought depressed him even more.

He felt weary to the bone, hollowed out as he slid behind the wheel and cranked the engine. God, he missed her already and it had only been a few minutes. How was he supposed to get over her after what they'd been through, what they'd shared last night?

Shifting into reverse, he waited for the cars behind

him to pass before backing out, using his mirrors. He turned the wheels, shifted into drive and glanced up, only to hit the brakes when he saw Trinity standing there in front of him. She stared at him, unmoving, her expression unreadable.

Stunned, he quickly put it in park and opened his door, his heart thudding. He climbed out and approached her slowly, an invisible cable squeezing his ribcage. Did this mean what he thought it did? Had she changed her mind?

As he started toward her, her expression shifted, the calm mask slipping. She looked bewildered, a little lost even and his heart turned over. "Hey," he said, wanting to grab her so bad he had to shove his hands into his pockets to keep from reaching for her. She looked ready to bolt. "What happened?"

She stared back at him for a long moment, the confusion and uncertainty on her face tearing at him. Then she lifted a shoulder and shook her head. "I couldn't do it."

Couldn't do what, get on the plane? A wild surge of hope exploded inside him.

She didn't move as he closed the distance between them, just kept watching him with those fathomless, deep blue eyes. There was fear there. Fear he wanted to wipe away forever. It was like she was afraid to come to him. Afraid to take that last step.

The hand holding the strap of her bag on her shoulder squeezed once and her throat worked as she swallowed. "I don't know what I'm doing," she confessed, her voice unsteady. "I've never done this before."

Unable to be this close and not touch her, Brody caught her free hand. "Done what?" he murmured, lifting his other hand to stroke his fingers across her cheek.

So damn soft. She was so beautiful and strong, but right now she was afraid and it floored him. She needed him and it shook her.

He wanted to gather her up in his arms and never let her go.

"I've never not been able to walk away," she whispered, looking so vulnerable it broke his heart.

Hell, she undid him without even trying. "I'm glad you didn't. Now God, just…come here." With a groan of sheer relief that came from deep in his chest he pulled her into his arms and hugged her tight.

Trinity wrapped her arms around his ribs and held on hard, plastering her body to his, as if she couldn't get close enough. It felt fucking incredible. He never wanted to let her go.

She gave a shuddering sigh. "What the hell did you do to me?" she accused, her cheek pressed to his chest.

"Same thing you did to me," he answered, not one damn bit sorry.

Raising her head, she met his eyes. Hope. That's what reflected back at him. "So what happens now?"

He smoothed a lock of hair away from her cheek. "Guess that depends on you." Because he was all in. She needed to decide whether she was or not.

Now her expression turned tormented. "I don't know what I want, I just know that I couldn't leave you. I don't…"

"Hey, shhh." He took her face between his hands, the need to comfort and reassure her overwhelming. "Don't look so scared, sweetheart. I'm right here and I'm not going anywhere." He rubbed his thumbs across her cheeks. "So what do you want?"

A sheen of tears glistened in her eyes and the sight pierced him. He knew for a fact she wouldn't let anyone else except maybe Briar see her this vulnerable. "You," she whispered, her voice cracking.

Warmth and longing and something a lot like love filled his chest until he thought it might burst. "Then I'm all yours."

As long as you're willing to be mine.

He didn't dare say it aloud, knowing that for her it would be too much too soon. The last thing he wanted was to spook her into running now that she'd finally reached out to him. But this was one hell of a start, and way more than he'd ever dreamed of having.

"I don't know how to do this. I don't know where we go from here." Her eyes practically begged him to give her the answer.

"Then how about I drive you back to my place and we just take this one day at a time, see what happens?"

Relief filled her expression, her posture easing. A tremulous smile spread across her face, the hope shining in her eyes as tangible as a touch. "That sounds perfect."

Yeah, it really did.

Epilogue

Three weeks later

Trinity fought the stab of disappointment that hit her when she checked her phone for what felt like the thousandth time in the past forty-eight hours. Brody hadn't responded to any of her texts. She'd even left him a voice message a few hours ago because she missed him so damn much, and still nothing.

It wasn't like him not to respond, not for this long. And she had a huge decision to make. One that would change the course of her life if she said yes. She couldn't say yes without talking to Brody first, however.

Sighing, she got up and headed to the fridge, telling herself to cope already. She'd been the one to pull away and fly back here rather than stay with him, so she could have time and space to think.

Careful what you wish for, Trin.

Well, she was now thoroughly sick of having time to herself to think. After some in-depth soul searching during the first week she'd been back in London, she'd come to the conclusion that her worst fears had been realized.

She'd fallen in love with him.

Not that she really knew what love looked like or felt like, but this had to be it. She'd never felt anything this strong, had never wanted to be with someone this badly. Being apart from him for this long made it feel like there was a hole inside her.

It wasn't just one thing she missed about him. They'd talked pretty much every day since she'd first given in and called him, rather than the other way around. She missed him like hell, missed just being next to him. She loved his strength and his integrity and his commitment to his job and his family.

Even the way he was moody in the morning before he had his coffee was a little adorable. He wasn't perfect, no one was, least of all her, but he was perfect for her. As unexpected and terrifying as that realization was, there was no disputing it.

She wanted to be with him. To wake up beside him every day. To come home to him at night, and—holy hell, she never thought she'd feel this way, but—maybe even spend the rest of her life with him.

Trouble was, she had no clue if he was ready to make that kind of leap and she had no intention of jumping unless she knew there was some kind of safety net waiting below to catch her. She'd told him she had to do this, to get some distance for clarity, to think about them together and be sure she could trust her heart, and he'd agreed to give her time.

The kitchen tile she'd picked out was cold against her bare feet. Her place was nice enough. She'd had the kitchen redone about six months ago to suit her tastes. Everything was in shades of white and cream, except for the rich mahogany floors throughout her condo. She'd bought and redecorated it with the aim of creating a safe, calming environment of tranquility for her to surround herself with between jobs.

Normally in her precious and rare hours of downtime she loved curling up on the couch in front of the gas fireplace to read or drink a cup of tea. Today her surroundings felt cold and sterile. Empty.

Because she was lonely.

She missed Brody so much it was a constant physical ache in the center of her chest. She was done with this whole lifestyle that she had once thought was so amazing and empowering, but was really just a cage. For years she'd put her country's needs before her own. Now she wanted a life for herself. She wanted to be *free*. And she wanted Brody.

It had been just over three weeks since she'd left the States. Three weeks since she'd finally forced herself to get on the damn plane and come back here to figure out what she wanted to do with the rest of her life. The offer she'd received yesterday seemed like it might be the answer to all her prayers.

In the end she'd stayed with Brody four more days beyond her first scheduled departure date. At the time she'd told herself it was mostly for convenience's sake, since they'd both had to attend interviews and meetings with Rycroft and other NSA officials during their investigation.

In reality, it was because she hadn't been strong enough to leave Brody. She'd left with the promise only that she'd think about what she wanted in terms of a relationship with him.

The answer had become crystal clear to her at the start of the second week, she'd just been too afraid to tell him. Hell, she'd even thought about just booking a flight and going back to Virginia to surprise him. Her deep-seated fear of rejection had stopped her cold.

Her life wasn't all loneliness and gray clouds though. Shortly after coming back to London, Rycroft had called to let her know he'd found out who the dirty CIA officer was.

No surprise to her, it turned out to be the contact she'd dealt with for the Salvatori job. He'd been arrested and charged, was currently awaiting trial and faced going to jail for the next twenty-five years. Rycroft said with the evidence she'd provided he was definitely getting convicted. In a few months she'd have to go there and testify. The only reason she wasn't dreading that was because it gave her the chance to see Brody again.

She perused the meager contents of her fridge, made a face when she realized just how little was in there. A few apples, some Greek yogurt and veggies when what she needed was a heaping bowl of fettuccini Alfredo or a homemade bread pudding with extra chocolate. She'd have to order some takeout.

Resigned, she grabbed her phone and headed back to the couch, called her favorite Italian place to order some fettuccini for delivery. When the phone dinged half an hour later with a new message, her pulse spiked. But it wasn't Brody texting. It was Briar.

More disappointment washed over her. She loved Briar but the only person she wanted to hear from right now wasn't responding for some reason. Brody had been given the green light to go back to work—to a desk job until he'd fully recovered—but he wasn't supposed to start until next Monday. Had he been called out somewhere and hadn't been able to tell her?

She snorted at herself. God, she was such a hypocrite. When she'd gone on jobs she hadn't told anyone where she was going. Of course, she'd never been involved with anyone before. Not to this extent.

Alex said he offered you the job. Are you going to

take it? Briar texted.

Trinity could easily picture her dancing on the spot with excitement as she typed it. *Haven't decided yet.*

She'd wanted to tell Brody first, feel him out in terms of what he thought, since taking the job would mean her moving to either Virginia or Maryland. She didn't think she could be that close to him and not see him.

It wasn't like they'd made any promises to each other or anything. He'd been careful not to push her on making any firm commitment, and dammit, it had worked because now she couldn't stand being apart from him. Four days of hot and heavy and a few harrowing situations together before that did not a relationship make.

Except it had sure felt like they'd been heading into a serious relationship over the past few weeks. At first when she'd come here she'd been determined to distance herself from him. He'd texted and called her a few times every day, and she always responded. Then she'd found she looked forward to hearing from him and had started to miss him.

Eventually she'd broken her cardinal rule about distancing herself from him and called him first. Since then they'd spoken on the phone at least once every day, sometimes lasting for hours. He filled her in on what was happening with his rehab, his team and his family. In turn she'd told him everything he wanted to know about her. He knew pretty much everything about her, except for the secrets she'd been sworn to keep about previous ops.

And now, for some reason, he wasn't answering her.

The flash of hurt and insecurity pissed her off. What the hell? She was being such a girl. Like one of those annoying female characters from the chick-flicks she hated so much, who sat around feeling lonely and sorry for herself while waiting lovesick by the phone for her man to call.

Gah. Brody had somehow turned her from a deadly and feared assassin into a freaking *girl*.

What's there to think about? Briar demanded. *Call him and tell him yes, then get your ass on a plane back here.*

Trinity smirked. *You wish.*

Hell yeah, I do.

A sharp rap sounded on her door.

Fettuccini time. She swiped her thumb across the screen of her phone and brought up her security app. The deliveryman stood with his back to the hidden video camera, facing the exterior wall of her courtyard garden.

Her heart skipped a beat when she took in the broad shoulders encased in a black leather jacket, his rain-slicked dark hair. He reminded her so much of Brody from the back.

Her breath caught when he half-turned and she saw his face. She dropped the phone onto the couch, was up and running for the door before she was even conscious of moving. Undoing all the locks, she yanked it open and stood there staring at Brody.

His face split into a warm, sexy smile. "Hey. You ordered Italian, apparently?" He held up the takeout bag.

Trinity didn't answer, she jumped. Literally threw herself into his arms and clung, wrapping her arms and legs around him.

Brody caught her, chuckled deep in his chest as he hugged her and walked them inside out of the rain, setting the takeout on her entry table without releasing her. "Wow, I guess this means you're happy to see me?"

She caught his face between her hands and kissed him. A hard, desperate, hungry kiss that made her ache all over. Made her want to rip all his clothes off and kiss every inch of him. It had been too long since she'd seen him, too long since she'd tasted him and felt his arms around her.

He leaned against the door to shut it, one hand cupping the back of her head and the other holding her rear, his mouth every bit as hungry as hers. After a minute she unwound her legs and set her feet on the floor, then ended the kiss to gaze up at him. "I can't believe you're here." It was the most romantic thing in the world, him surprising her this way.

God, maybe part of her *was* "that" girl from the chick-flick movie, and maybe there wasn't anything wrong about that at all.

His eyes were filled with silent laughter. "I can't believe I waited this long to fly over here if this is my welcome. I was only giving you your damn space so I didn't scare you away."

"I don't scare easy." She smiled, but there were tears burning her eyes. "God I've missed you," she whispered.

His expression sobered and he cupped the side of her face in one wide palm. "Did you seriously think I was planning to let you walk away and forget me?"

Biting her lower lip, she shrugged, suddenly vulnerable and unsure. "I wasn't sure what you'd do."

His eyes widened at that but then he frowned. "Sweetheart, there's no way in hell I'd let you go without a fight."

The endearment and the conviction in his voice made her go all gooey inside.

"And I'm only letting your whole doubt thing slide because I know you don't trust what's going on between us. That's why I flew here, because I have something to say and it needed to be said face-to-face. Now come here." With that he grabbed her hand and towed her to the couch. "Nice place," he commented as he sat, dragging her down to straddle his lap.

She set her hands on his shoulders. To hell with her place, she couldn't stand the suspense another minute. "You didn't return my texts or calls for the past two days. Was it because you were coming here?"

He nodded, slid his hands into her hair. "I got your voicemail once I landed in Heathrow. I didn't call back because I wanted to surprise you."

Aw. "Mission accomplished."

Something shifted in his gaze, something hot and possessive. "Not yet."

That sounded borderline cryptic, but she let it go. "So what did you want to say?" she prompted, heart thudding with a mixture of hope and excitement.

"You first. That was a lot of messages, for you. What did you want to tell me about?"

"I got a job offer yesterday."

"Oh?" His gaze turned knowing. "Anything interesting?"

He already knew. She had to smile. "Rycroft offered me a job working with him and Briar."

He nodded, confirming her suspicions. "And?"

"And that's why I was calling you. I wanted to know what you thought."

"What do *you* think?" he countered.

She shrugged, resisted the urge to squirm under the force of that dark gaze. And it was damn hard to think or have this conversation when she was straddling his lap and she wanted him so damn bad.

"That would depend on us. How you see things…progressing between us in the future." A part of her cringed as she said it, hating the feeling of exposure. He could literally crush her heart with the wrong answer.

"Ah." He curved his hand around the back of her neck, the possessive vibe to it making her shiver inside. She loved the way he touched her, and especially the way he took charge in bed. "That brings me to why I flew all the way over here."

"Just tell me," she blurted, annoyance taking over her curiosity. Here she was, desperate for the man, for some kind of promise, and he was making her wait.

A slow, sexy grin spread across his face. "You stubborn, gorgeous thing. I came here to tell you to your face that I love you."

She stared at him, hear heart seizing for a moment before it swelled to double its normal size.

"And I also came here to try and talk you into moving back to the States. With me, into my place."

To her horror, tears flooded her eyes. She choked back a sniffle, cupped his face in her hands. "You love me?" she quavered.

No one had ever loved her before.

Not her parents. Not her trainers and certainly not the people who should have protected her from the man who'd raped her. Briar and Georgia loved her in their own way, but it wasn't the same as this. Brody's admission shook her, his love filling her entire body with warmth.

He nodded. "Yeah. And I wanted to hold you like this and look into your eyes when I said it."

Her insides began to quake. Could this be real? Could a man like him really love her and want to make a life with her? It seemed like more than she deserved, given what she'd done for all these years.

He's mine. The words felt unbelievable, and yet so right.

Staring into his eyes, a sense of security and peace wrapped around her. If she jumped, he would catch her. He would never let her fall. And he would also protect her with his dying breath.

She would do the same for him, without hesitation. So there was only one answer she could give him, even if it was terrifying to voice it aloud.

She smiled at him, pure joy exploding inside her. "I love you too." So much it took her breath away.

Triumph flashed in his eyes. His grip on her nape tightened and he gave a soft growl as he pulled her down for a slow, hot kiss that melted her insides.

Just as she was about to slide into a puddle on his lap, he broke the kiss and peered up at her, a slight frown drawing his eyebrows together. "So this means you're going to move in with me and take the job, right? Say the words, Trin."

Admitting she loved him had been the hardest thing she'd ever done. This part was easy. "God help you, but yes. I am," she murmured, and covered his lips with hers.

—The End—

Thank you for reading BRODY'S VOW. I really hope you enjoyed it and that you'll consider leaving a review at one of your favorite online retailers. It's a great way to help other readers discover new books.

If you liked BRODY'S VOW and would like to read more, turn the page for a list of my other books. And if you don't want to miss any future releases, please join my newsletter:

http://kayleacross.com/v2/newsletter/

Complete Booklist

ROMANTIC SUSPENSE

Colebrook Siblings Trilogy
Brody's Vow

Hostage Rescue Team Series
Marked
Targeted
Hunted
Disavowed
Avenged
Exposed
Seized
Wanted
Betrayed
Reclaimed

Titanium Security Series
Ignited
Singed
Burned
Extinguished
Rekindled

Bagram Special Ops Series
Deadly Descent
Tactical Strike
Lethal Pursuit
Danger Close
Collateral Damage

Suspense Series

Out of Her League
Cover of Darkness
No Turning Back
Relentless
Absolution

PARANORMAL ROMANCE
Empowered Series
Darkest Caress

HISTORICAL ROMANCE
The Vacant Chair

EROTIC ROMANCE (writing as *Callie Croix*)
Deacon's Touch
Dillon's Claim
No Holds Barred
Touch Me
Let Me In
Covert Seduction

Acknowledgements

A shout out to all my wonderful readers, for supporting this new series.

And as always, a huge thanks to my editing team (including Sandra, thanks for pinch hitting on this one!), cover artist, formatter and DH, for all their help in whipping this baby into shape. It takes a village!

About the Author

NY Times and USA Today Bestselling author Kaylea Cross writes edge-of-your-seat military romantic suspense. Her work has won many awards and has been nominated for both the Daphne du Maurier and the National Readers' Choice Awards. A Registered Massage Therapist by trade, Kaylea is also an avid gardener, artist, Civil War buff, Special Ops aficionado, belly dance enthusiast and former nationally-carded softball pitcher. She lives in Vancouver, BC with her husband and family.

You can visit Kaylea at www.kayleacross.com. If you would like to be notified of future releases, please join her newsletter:

http://kayleacross.com/v2/newsletter/

CPSIA information can be obtained at www.ICGtesting.com
Printed in the USA
LVOW11s1840040916

503188LV00005B/153/P

9 781535 422444